PRESCRIPTION FOR HAPPINESS

From their very first meeting, sparks fly between Rose and Matthew. But they soon discover they have a lot in common — both are coping with loss, and both have a parentless child to love and care for. Their young nieces become best friends, and want nothing more than for all of them to become a family. But even though Rose and Matthew help each other through tough times, neither of them are sure they can get over their past hurts to love again . . .

PATRICIA POSNER

PRESCRIPTION FOR HAPPINESS

Complete and Unabridged

LINFORD
Leicester

First published in Great Britain in 2006

First Linford Edition
published 2007

British Library CIP Data

Posner, Patricia
Prescription for happiness.—Large print ed.—
Linford romance library
1. Love stories
2. Large type books
I. Title
823.9′2 [F]

ISBN 978–1–84617–874–0

Published by
F. A. Thorpe (Publishing)
Anstey, Leicestershire

Set by Words & Graphics Ltd.
Anstey, Leicestershire
Printed and bound in Great Britain by
T. J. International Ltd., Padstow, Cornwall

This book is printed on acid-free paper

A Harrowing Experience

'I don't want to come with you. You can't make me — you're not my daddy!'

The child's high-pitched words, followed by harsh sobbing, echoed around the deserted school playground and made Rose's hair stand on end and her blood run cold.

With a speed she didn't know she was capable of, she made for the open gates and catapulted herself from the top of the short flight of steps down to the pavement below. She landed an arm's length away from the sobbing child and the man who was moving away from the open door of a metallic green Range Rover.

They reached out for the little girl at the same time.

'What the heck do you think you're doing?' rasped the man, straightening up and glaring down at Rose.

'I think you're the one who should answer that question,' she replied forcefully, hoping and praying that one of the passing cars would stop or that someone — anyone — would come along.

But school had finished more than twenty minutes ago. Rose knew that because she'd been in the head teacher's office at the time and had stood by the window watching the children making their noisy way across the playground to the school gates.

'I don't want to go with him. I don't want a puppy, I want my daddy!' wailed the little girl and she turned round to bury her head against Rose's stomach.

Rose's hands stroked the tousled black curls but she kept her gaze firmly fixed on the man's face. Dark eyebrows crinkled into a worried frown over brown eyes fringed with even darker lashes.

Well, he's bound to look worried, isn't he, she told herself, as he ran his fingers through his hair.

'Look, this isn't what you think,' he said. 'Ask her. Just ask her who I am.'

'She doesn't want to go with you, whoever you are. You're obviously not her father and — '

'Sweetheart.' He touched the little girl's heaving shoulders. 'Tell the lady who I am or I'll be in big trouble.'

The only response from the child was louder and more frantic sobbing. The Range Rover's rear door was still open. Feeling herself going hot and cold, Rose started edging herself and the child slowly backwards, her one thought to get up the steps, across the playground and into the school building.

'Rosie, what on earth's going on here?'

Rose spun round with a gasp of disbelief. Rosie? Hannah was the only person who had ever called her that! But she knew it couldn't be her sister who'd spoken.

Hannah was dead . . .

3

She closed her eyes briefly against the pain — this was no time for personal feelings. But when she opened them again it was to see a plump, grey-haired woman looking, not at her, but down at the child clasped to her body.

So this little girl is called Rosie, realised Rose. She spoke urgently to the woman: 'Look, will you go and phone the police? This man is trying to persuade — '

'Oh, for goodness' sake!' the man exploded. 'Ellen, tell this . . . this person who you are and who I am and see if that will convince her that I'm not trying to abduct Rosie.'

'I'm the school-crossing attendant, love.'

Rose just glared. True, if this Ellen really was the school lollipop lady, she would know all the children and all the people who came to collect them from school. But . . .

'All the school-crossing attendants I've ever seen wear a yellow coat and carry a lollipop pole,' snapped Rose.

4

An impatient muttering came from the man behind her. Rose ignored it and waited for the woman's response.

'My afternoon stint finished at three-thirty; I've just been to dump my gear in the shop over there. This little mite . . . ' The woman's eyes clouded and she shook her head.

'Ellen, get on with it. Just tell her who I am and how I know Rosie.'

'He's Rosie's uncle, love,' said Ellen. 'Rosie lives with him and her auntie now. You see — '

'If that's true, why is Rosie refusing to go with him and why wasn't he here when school finished?' demanded Rose.

'Rosie stayed behind after school to practise the hymn she'll be singing solo at the Harvest Festival in a couple of weeks. That's right, isn't it, Rosie?' Ellen touched the little girl's shoulder. 'You told me all about it this morning, didn't you?'

The only response was a muffled sob.

Rose glanced at the man. 'Why didn't

you tell me any of that, yourself?' she challenged.

'Even if you'd given me the chance, would you have believed me?' he asked, quirking an eyebrow.

'No, I don't think I would. In fact . . . ' Rose looked at the woman again, 'I don't know if . . . ' She gnawed at her lower lip.

'Ellen, I do believe you've been cast in the role of my wicked accomplice. Go over to the shop and fetch Jim and Mary, will you? We'll be here all night otherwise.'

He turned to her then and said, 'Will you believe that Ellen and I aren't in some awful plot together if the shopkeepers vouch for us?'

Rosie made a quick decision. 'I think the best way to sort this out is to go into the school,' she stated and he nodded.

'You're right. That would be the best thing to do. I'm sure even you would accept Miss Peplow's word.'

Rose didn't like that 'even you', but

6

she did recognise a sudden air of authority about the man as he moved to slam the rear door shut. Authority and confidence. It looked as if he really was the child's uncle, after all. Nevertheless . . .

'Come on, Rosie,' she urged. 'We'll go and see Miss Peplow.'

Rosie gulped, removed her face from Rose's stomach and tilted her head back to look up at her. 'It's all right. I'll go with Uncle Matt. I don't want to but . . . but I know I can't have my daddy or my mummy.' Her eyes swam with fresh tears. 'They're in Heaven, you see. I asked Uncle Matt if he would go and get them back and he 'splained how you can't get anyone back when they've gone to Heaven. But . . . '

The little girl's mouth trembled and tears cascaded down her blotchy cheeks; Rose felt an ominous pricking in her own eyes as the child continued, ' . . . but singing the harvest hymn reminded me of them so much.' She shuffled round. 'It was Daddy's favourite hymn, Uncle Matt.'

'Oh, Rosie, love.' He opened his arms wide and as his niece went to him he scooped her up and hugged her tightly to him.

His dark brown eyes were suspiciously bright as he looked across at Rose and demanded grittily, 'I presume you'll make no fuss if I take Rosie home now?'

'No, no. I'm . . . I'm — '

'Forget it.' He cut harshly across her apology as he opened the rear door and placed the still sniffling Rosie gently on the back seat. He kissed the top of her head and fastened her safety belt.

'Call it your good deed for the day,' he added to Rose as he straightened up and closed the door. 'Misguided though it was.'

A gamut of conflicting emotions warred inside Rose; indignation, embarrassment, sympathy born of empathy — she knew all too well how it felt to lose loved ones and to be responsible for a parentless child — and a longing to put her arms around Rosie's uncle, to offer comfort.

But, she realised bleakly, she'd left it too late to even try to apologise again. While she'd been standing there swamped by her emotions, he'd started the Range Rover and was now about to join the steady trickle of traffic.

★ ★ ★

Rose turned to look at Ellen. 'How . . . how did her . . . ?' She broke off. 'Sorry — it's nothing to do with me,' she murmured.

'Motorway pile-up. Killed outright they say.' Ellen briskly answered the unfinished question. 'You weren't to know. And Rosie *was* carrying on, poor mite.' She sniffed and blinked hard. 'They'll be missed a lot. They were solicitors with offices in the town centre; they held a free advice clinic every couple of months or so. I've never seen the church so packed as it was for their funeral service.'

Pulling a handkerchief from up her sleeve, Ellen blew her nose before continuing, 'Little Rosie stayed dry-eyed all through — hurting too much to cry, I suppose. If you ask me, she's just starting to unbottle her grief now, poor little soul.'

'Singing her dad's favourite hymn probably acted as a trigger,' Rose said quietly.

Ellen sighed. 'Most folk say her uncle, being used to dealing with bereavement and all, should be able to see her through the bad times better than most. Personally, I reckon that could make it harder for him.'

Rose nodded. 'It is heart-breaking dealing with a child's grief.'

There was a moment's silence.

'Right,' said Ellen brusquely, as though regretting having spoken so forthrightly, 'I'd best be on my way. My George likes his tea on the table when he comes home from work.'

Rose nodded and took a deep, shaky

breath. Awash with pain, she reflected bleakly how much she and Rosie's uncle seemed to have in common. But at least he had a wife to share the responsibility with, whereas she . . .

'I'm all alone,' Rose whispered, allowing herself a moment to wallow.

Then her spine stiffened. Not true, Rose Winter, she admonished silently. You've got good friends — lots of them. And as for Stephen, it's a good thing I found out how . . . how heartless he could be. I'm much better off without him. Pull yourself together and get on with your plans. Today is an important day. Pippa's schooling is arranged and . . .

Suddenly the last words Ellen had spoken registered with her brain: 'Likes his tea on the table . . . '

Tea. Surely it wasn't that time already? Rose dashed a fugitive tear from her cheek, looked at her watch and gasped. Her interview! She'd be late. Not only late but untidy too, she acknowledged ruefully as she hurried to the side street where she'd parked her car.

Her sprint across the playground would have done nothing for her fly-away hair, her white blouse felt damp from Rosie's tears and, she noted, glancing down, not only was it damp but crumpled and slightly grubby.

In her haste to unlock the car door she dropped the bunch of keys she'd fumbled out of her bag. As she bent down to retrieve them, she noticed a thin white line running all the way up one leg of her black tights.

'Maybe I'd be best just not going for the interview,' she muttered as she unlocked and opened the car door. 'I won't stand a chance now.' Arriving late with untidy hair, sticky face, stained and crumpled blouse and a laddered stocking — hardly a suitable applicant for the position of Practice Nurse!

But she wanted the job, didn't she?

Her usual determination took over. After a hasty look round, she got into the car and wriggled out of her tights.

'Whew!' she groaned thankfully. 'At least I managed that without anyone coming along!'

Reaching for the first aid box she always kept in the car, she rummaged for some cleansing wipes for her face and hands, then delved into her handbag for a brush and ran it through her hair.

There was no time to repair her light make-up.

'That'll have to do,' she muttered, switching on the ignition.

She eased her car out of the side street, and felt a spurt of anger as she drove past the spot where her confrontation with Rosie's uncle had taken place. He could have at least tried telling her who he was!

Still, she acknowledged with compassion, he was probably upset to see Rosie in such a state and wasn't thinking straight.

Just as well he couldn't, I suppose, she mused. Being a solicitor, he could have sued me for slander.

She felt a hot flush of embarrassment and discomfiture as she realised exactly what she'd more or less accused him of. More, not less. What that poor man must have felt! She'd have to find out where his office was and, tomorrow, she'd go and apologise to him.

There was no time to dwell on that any more now, though, since she'd reached her destination. Rose took a deep, calming breath as she drew up on the forecourt of Morden Health Centre.

The Interview

'Eight minutes late,' she murmured. Not bad, considering. Maybe nobody would notice her bare legs and grubby blouse, she prayed as she walked towards the modern, single-storey building. And as for her lateness, well, she could only apologise. She certainly wasn't going to explain what had made her late.

Nevertheless, Rose felt rather flustered when she reached the reception desk. The receptionist, who was wearing a badge that announced her name to be Linda, smiled when Rose gave her name and said she was here for an interview.

'I'm sorry, I'm a bit late,' she added.

'Doctors Sinclair and Gordon are waiting for you, Miss Winter,' said Linda. Then, as Rose sighed and rolled her eyes, she gave a sympathetic smile and continued, 'They're waiting for Dr

15

Knight, too. He phoned through to say he'd been delayed.'

In a much louder voice, she continued, 'So sorry I had to keep you waiting, Miss Winter — that was my elderly next-door neighbour on the phone, giving me her shopping list. She kept changing her mind about what she wanted me to get.'

Linda's eye closed in the slightest of winks as she continued brightly, 'Here's Dr Sinclair, coming to see why I haven't shown you through yet. I was just explaining to Miss Winter, Doctor, why I held her up. Mrs Crabtree phoned to — '

'I heard, Linda.' The voice was calm and pleasant and with a grateful look at Linda for covering up for her, Rose turned to face its owner.

'Dr Sinclair.' He introduced himself with a smile and Rose smiled back. The doctor was small and plumpish with a mass of thick brown hair and the bluest eyes Rose had ever seen. He looks like everyone's favourite uncle, she thought as they shook hands.

'Come through and meet Dr Gordon,' he said. 'Our third partner, Dr Knight, has been held up, but I'm sure he won't object if we make a start without him.'

He led her down the corridor facing the reception desk.

'Dr Knight only joined us six months ago,' he explained. 'There's been a fair amount of building in Morden recently — old mills being turned into flats and a couple of new housing developments, so we've had to expand to cope with additional patients. That's why we need an extra Practice Nurse to join the two existing full-time nurses.'

Rose followed him into a room which looked like a friendly, welcoming sitting-room in someone's house — though the tall, aloof-looking brunette standing shuffling papers at a large oak table didn't look so friendly or welcoming.

'Dr Gordon.' Rose was informed. 'Audrey, Miss Winter was kept waiting while Linda was taking a phone call.'

'Shall we get on with it now?' Dr Gordon said crisply, indicating for Rose to take a seat. 'The Well Woman Clinic is due to start in an hour,' she added pointedly.

'We see patients earlier than usual on Tuesday afternoons,' Dr Sinclair explained. 'If we're lucky we get an hour's break afterwards before the clinic.'

'I think we could go into practice and clinic times once Miss Winter has answered our questions,' stated Dr Gordon with a scarcely concealed impatience.

Rose breathed in deeply and faced the two doctors, ready for the interview to begin.

'You say in your covering letter you're about to move to Morden,' Audrey Gordon began. 'We wouldn't like to think you applied for this position as a stop-gap until you can find a full-time post elsewhere in the area.'

Rose noticed the reproachful look

Dr Sinclair cast at his partner. The statement had been straight to the point and rather harshly put, perhaps, but Rose could appreciate the reasoning behind it. True, she'd also explained in the letter why working part-time would suit her, but Dr Gordon may not have had time to read all of it.

'I can assure you I will not be looking for a full-time position,' Rose said firmly. 'That was one reason I applied for this post — because it's only part-time. My other reasons were the health centre being only about a quarter of an hour away from where I'll be living, and the size of the practice.'

She glanced quickly at Dr Sinclair. 'Although you've had to expand, it still seems as if it's small enough to be personal and friendly, but large enough to offer a variety of specialist clinics where my qualifications could be put to use.'

'Yes, I see from your CV that as well as being experienced in general treatment room activities and cervical smear tests, you have vaccination training, a Family Planning Certificate and your Diploma in Asthma. Your qualifications could certainly be put to use,' he commented with a smile. 'And in your last position, you used the same computer system as we have here. That's good.'

'Any experience with drug dependants?' Dr Gordon asked.

'I worked at an inner-city practice,' Rose told her.

'No experience with farming related ailments then?'

'I've dressed plenty of dog bites and given anti-tetanus jabs, treated flea-bites and nits and many a wound caused by broken glass and rusty metal.' The reply wasn't without dry humour, although Rose had a strong feeling that Audrey Gordon had already decided against her.

Audrey Gordon nodded. 'Not quite what I was thinking of, but point taken.'

'Besides which, Audrey, Miss Winter won't be expected to diagnose,' her partner pointed out gently.

'That's just as well,' came a voice from the doorway. 'I think Miss Winter would be likely to come to the wrong conclusion.'

Rose recognised the voice immediately and felt the colour draining from her cheeks. What on earth was Rosie's uncle doing here? Had he come to vet her? She'd heard that some hospitals and GPs included solicitors on the interview board to assess an applicant's suitability.

Well, that's me done for, she thought wryly.

$\star$ $\star$ $\star$

Dr Sinclair pushed back his chair and got to his feet. 'Matthew, glad you made it.'

He looked at Rose and smiled, 'Miss Winter, this our third partner, Dr Knight.'

'Doctor? But Ellen said you were a solicitor!' Rose spoke without thinking.

'At least . . . ' She hesitated, her brow crumpled in an effort to remember exactly what Ellen had said.

'Another wrong conclusion, hmm?'

'What is all this about wrong conclusions, Matt?' Dr Sinclair looked bewildered. 'Have you and Miss Winter met?'

Dr Matthew Knight didn't take his eyes from Rose's face. 'We haven't been formally introduced,' he said. 'Your interview was for four o'clock, Miss Winter. Did you manage to get here on time?'

'Not quite,' Rose murmured, wishing she could slide under the table and disappear.

'And did you explain why you were late?'

Unexpectedly it was Audrey Gordon who answered that. 'Miss Winter was only a few minutes late, Matt. And that was mainly due to Linda keeping her waiting while she took a phone call. Besides . . . ' She tapped her watch and smiled up at him.

'Ah, yes, I'm afraid I suffered a delay.'

There was a teasing note in his voice, Rose thought in surprise, and as he sat down on the opposite side of the table, she wondered if she'd imagined the small smile he threw in her direction before turning to his partners.

'Where were you up to?' he asked blandly.

'I think we've more or less covered most things, haven't we, Audrey?' said Dr Sinclair.

'Not quite. In her letter, Miss Winter mentions an interest in alternative therapies.' Dr Gordon looked and sounded disapproving.

'I've an interest in complementary therapies, certainly,' Rose said. 'I only wish more doctors would recognise that CTs can be beneficial alongside conventional medicine in certain cases.'

It was a challenging statement and she knew it. She might have made it in a gentler manner if she'd thought there was any chance of being offered the post. But it was clear that any chance she may have had was doomed with the advent of Rosie's uncle.

'Would you care to enlarge on that, Miss Winter?' Matthew Knight's tone was provocative.

Rose met his dark gaze full on. If this man thought provocation would fluster her, he had another thought coming. 'Certainly.'

His fleeting expression of — could it possibly be admiration? — swayed her composure for a second. Then she titled her chin defiantly.

'A recent report for Macmillan Cancer Relief mentions acupuncture being used to ease the side effects of treatment,' she stated. 'And some midwives also train as acupuncturists because it can help with certain antenatal problems, it may offer some relief in labour and can be useful with some postnatal complications, too.'

She looked at him to gauge his reaction. He gazed back impassively. Rose shrugged mentally and went on: 'Then there's aromatherapy, reflexology and bodywork therapies — '

'I take it you're talking about massage?' He was half-smiling now and, to her horror, Rose felt herself blushing.

She swallowed and forced the words out of her mouth. 'Lots of mums find baby massage helpful. It can make a baby feel calmer, therefore parents feel better.'

'That makes sense,' said Dr Sinclair.

His deep, kindly voice had a steadying effect on Rose, and reminded her that there were two other doctors in the room.

Looking at them, instead of Dr Knight, she went on, 'If a mother's breast-feeding, a calm baby can help her produce more milk. Infant massage is helpful, too. I often massage my young niece when . . . '

Rose's words tailed off, she'd been about to say, 'when she's crying for her mum and dad,' but remembering Matthew Knight's circumstances, she concluded with ' . . . when she's finding it hard to get to sleep.'

'So you practise what you preach?' said Dr Knight.

'If the circumstances warrant it, yes, I do,' Rose replied.

'I see. So, is there anything else we want to ask Miss Winter?' Audrey Gordon asked her partners.

Dr Knight picked up Rose's CV and scanned it quickly.

His eyes were bleak when he looked up and said, 'I see from this that you've almost completed a two-year diploma course in counselling, Miss Winter.'

Rose nodded. She'd listed the course contents, Grief and Bereavement Counselling amongst them. Was Rosie's grief, or his own, the reason for his question? Her heart went out to him but she regarded him steadily.

'What made you decide to take the course? Any particular reason?'

'Three years ago, we . . . ' Her voice faltered momentarily, then she started again. 'Three years ago, my parents lost their lives in a hotel fire. As well as the

26

shock of their death and the natural grief, there were my feelings of guilt. You see, I'd encouraged them to take the holiday. My sister, who hadn't wanted them to go — well, she miscarried. Not that she blamed me. Hannah isn't . . . wasn't . . . '

Rose came to a halt and fought to control herself. She hadn't yet come to terms with the death of her sister and brother-in-law. If it wasn't for Dr Knight's presence, or her knowledge of the situation he was in with his niece, she might have mentioned this more recent tragedy as well. But she couldn't, not now. He might think she was playing for his sympathy.

So, with only a slight quiver in her voice, she finished with the words, 'Anyway, counselling helped me then, so . . . '

'So you decided you'd like to be in a position to help others the way you'd been helped?' Dr Sinclair asked gruffly, and Rose nodded.

'How near the end of your course are

you, Miss Winter?' Dr Knight asked brusquely.

Audrey Gordon spoke before Rose had a chance to reply. 'You're thinking we could hold a Counselling Clinic, Matt?'

She sounded disapproving, but Dr Knight was quick to put his point over. 'A great number of our patients suffer from depression, Audrey. And alcoholism and drug dependency. Some of our single-parent families find it hard to cope with life. With the best will in the world, we don't have time to really talk to them when they come to see us.'

'We send quite a few for counselling,' Dr Sinclair put in, nodding thoughtfully. 'Some of those patients would react more favourably to a familiar face on familiar premises.'

'This room would be ideal.' Rose spoke without thinking. 'It's friendly and relaxing. It was my first impression when I walked in.'

'We haven't given Miss Winter a chance to answer my question yet,' Dr

Knight pointed out. 'How near the end of your course are you, Miss Winter?'

'I'm just waiting for my tutor's comments on my last assignment, Dr Knight. In other words, waiting to see if I get a pass grade.'

'Then you'll be able to use Dip CPC after your name?'

Rose nodded.

'I don't wish to denigrate what Miss Winter could offer us, Matt,' said Dr Gordon, 'but could we stick to more relevant details for now?'

'I think this is relevant, Audrey. What I'm getting at is that perhaps Miss Winter will want to put her skills to use in a more lucrative way if she successfully completes her course.'

He looked back to Rose. 'Is it merely coincidence that you've applied for a part-time position just as you're hoping to have letters after your name? Could it be you're thinking of private counselling as a side-line?'

Rose felt angry tears at the back of her eyes, felt the tide of hot colour coursing her cheeks. Hadn't he read her covering letter, either?

'Now who's jumping to conclusions?' she demanded. 'I think it's diabolical when a patient needing help sometimes has to pay for it in order to be seen sooner. And,' she added, 'those who can't afford to pay might change their mind about seeing someone if they have to wait even two or three days for an appointment.'

She drew in a harsh breath then continued: 'All practices should make sure they have someone with a diploma in counselling and offer a regular Counselling Clinic. Not only could a patient be seen quickly if it was necessary, there'd be the added security of knowing they could attend the clinic on a regular basis as well.'

'I tend to agree with you there,' said Matthew Knight. 'But — '

Rose cut across anything else he might have said. 'Oh, yes, there's always a 'but' when someone has the audacity to suggest there's room for improvement in a doctors' practice.'

She turned her glare on Audrey Gordon. 'You asked if I had any experience of farming-related ailments. Even though there weren't any actual cases of foot and mouth in Morden when the disease broke out a couple of years ago, I'm sure it affected farming families here in other ways. Emotionally as well as financially. And I do realise counselling can't help shortage of cash, but maybe it could help people to try and cope with it.'

★ ★ ★

Her outburst was met with a stunned silence, broken eventually by Dr Gordon. 'Well,' she said, 'you've certainly made your views on counselling extremely clear.'

If she's waiting for an apology, it'll be a long wait, Rose thought.

But the doctor was gathering her sheets of paper together. 'I'm afraid,' she said, 'that, as usual, time is against us. I'd just like to know when you'd be free to start should you be offered the position? I see you've already worked your notice.'

'I'm moving in over the weekend. I've put my present and my new address on the covering letter.' Rose's feeling of relief at being able to make that statement temporarily overrode all other feelings.

When they'd been killed, her sister and brother-in-law had only been two days away from moving into a farmhouse in the hills above Morden on the borders of Lancashire and Yorkshire.

Rose had spent a fraught two months waiting to see if the landlord of that property would waive his 'no single-parent families' rule and transfer the lease Hannah and Richard had negotiated to her. She was still faced with having to purchase the property when the six months' lease was up — or move out. But, hopefully, by then Richard's business would be sold and there would be enough money for a deposit.

'So you'd be free ... ?' Audrey Gordon prompted impatiently.

'I'd be free a week from today,' Rose replied flatly.

There had been no mention of how the twenty-five hours would be broken down, no discussion of actual duties. And no offer to show her around. Just the standard, polite way to end an interview.

'Well, Miss Winter,' Dr Sinclair leaned forward. 'You've answered all our questions with patience and put your points of view over with fervour. We'll be in touch with you in a few days, once we've seen all the applicants.' He stood up to accompany her to the door. 'We'll let you know either way,' he said kindly.

Rose forced herself to walk as naturally as possible down the corridor when what she really felt like doing was flouncing off in a temper. Underneath her temper, though, was an understanding of Matthew Knight's feelings.

The upsetting scene with his niece

would have only added to his own scars. Seeing her again so unexpectedly and so soon after Rosie's outburst wouldn't have helped allay his hurt and despair. Rose sighed. She just hoped his wife was able to help him and little Rosie cope with everything.

'How did it go?' asked Linda as Rose arrived in Reception.

'They'll let me know after they've seen all the applicants,' Rose answered diplomatically. 'Thank you for covering up for me being late,' she said with a smile. 'At least that didn't blot my copy book.'

She made her way to her car, despondent.

'Ah, well,' she thought. 'There'll be other jobs.'

about his feelings, his reasons for doing things?'

Annoyed with herself, she walked to the sink to wash her hands, then reached for a knife and began chopping tomatoes fiercely.

★ ★ ★

Lucy returned a few seconds later and Rose could tell at once that her godmother had something to convey.

'Is it Pippa?' Rose demanded urgently. 'That was Abigail on the phone, wasn't it!'

'Nothing drastic,' Lucy reassured her quickly. 'Just that Pippa has chosen which goat she wants. It's a small Saanen called Grizelda. But Pippa seems to have set her heart on having Grizelda *and* her kid. Abigail asked me to warn you.'

'Something tells me that isn't all.' Rose regarded the older woman intently. 'Is Pippa's leg hurting?'

The ligaments in Pippa's right leg

had been badly strained in the accident that had killed her parents.

'Abigail overheard Pippa telling Topsy — that's what she's named the kid, by the way — all about the crash. Did you know,' Lucy asked carefully, 'that Pippa thinks the accident was her fault?'

'What?' Rose grabbed the nearest stool and sat down with a thud. 'What exactly happened?' she asked. 'What led up to it?'

'Apparently, Pippa was watching Topsy and Grizelda playing. Abigail says when Topsy bleats it sounds as if she's laughing.' Lucy gave a weak smile. 'Topsy was chasing Grizelda and let out a really excited bleat.

'As far as Abigail can recall,' she continued, 'Grizelda sort of glanced back to look at Topsy and the next second ran into a stationary tractor. She wasn't hurt and both she and Pippa laughed at the incident.'

'But?' asked Rose.

'But later, Topsy went into the barn

Concern About Pippa

Actually, thought Rose as she drove, they probably weren't going to offer me the job anyway — even before Matthew Knight arrived and gave off disapproving vibes.

'I suspect I was a bit too emphatic about working part-time — I probably gave the impression I wouldn't be willing, or able, to put in any extra hours,' she told the teddy bear sitting on the passenger seat. She'd bought the bear for Pippa when she'd called in at a newsagent's near the health centre for a nursing magazine. After that interview, she'd have to start browsing the job advertisements again.

Maybe she should have mentioned Pippa . . . though she had said in her letter that the move was due to family bereavement and she now had her niece to care for.

As Rose joined the queue of traffic which had come to a halt at the temporary, and-slow-to-change, traffic lights, her thoughts turned to just one doctor. Matthew Knight. Had he really given off disapproving vibes? Perhaps she was reading something into his attitude that wasn't there because she was embarrassed by what had happened earlier?

No, no, she wasn't. His first comment was that she'd be likely to come to wrong conclusions. Rose groaned aloud; she'd proved how right he was with her stupid remark about him being a solicitor.

Understandably Matthew Knight wouldn't want to let someone who seemingly leapt to wrong conclusions loose on his patients. And, in a roundabout sort of way, he had let his partners see that. He wasn't to know that Dr Gordon at least had already decided against her before he'd joined them.

He didn't have to go on the way he

did about counselling or imply you'd be taking it up as a lucrative sideline, said her inner voice.

That was because the 'Grief and Bereavement' bit had hit a raw nerve and hurt, Rose argued back.

She tried, and failed, to ignore the same little voice asking why she was making excuses for him. It was nothing to do with feeling that she could see into his soul whenever she met his chocolate brown eyes — nothing to do with wanting to comfort him, to hold him close to ease away his hurt and tension.

'Where did that thought come from?' she demanded of her silent passenger. 'He's got a wife to do that.' And she had enough on her plate coping with her own grief and looking after Pippa; trying to make her little world a happier place.

At least she'd managed to sort out Pippa's schooling. She felt sure her niece would settle in well even though she'd missed the first three weeks of term. And she was taking her to spend the morning there the next day, before starting full-time the following week.

She wouldn't let Pippa know, yet, that she hadn't got the job. It would only worry her — especially as Rose had told her she wasn't upset about leaving her old job because she was looking forward to starting this new one. Hopefully, she'd be able to keep the conversation on Pippa's new school.

The demanding hooting of car horns made her realise that the lights had changed; she engaged gear, then moved forward.

★   ★   ★

When Rose finally arrived at her godmother's house where she'd left her niece, Pippa wasn't there.

'I took her round to see Abigail and Pippa decided she wanted to spend the afternoon with her and Thomas,' said Lucy, leading the way into the kitchen. 'Seeing as Abigail and Thomas are coming here for a meal when they've been to the Animal Rescue . . . '

'You mean you let slip where Abigail and Thomas were going,' Rose accused her godmother laughingly. 'Pippa thinks it's fantastic that Thomas is the Animal Rescue's vet. Naturally she wouldn't miss the opportunity of going with them. I only hope she doesn't set her heart on giving a donkey or a pig a home. The thought of coping with the goat and chickens I've promised her is bad enough. Goodness' knows what . . . '

'You're babbling, Rose,' her godmother returned calmly. 'I have a feeling it's just as well Pippa isn't here. Sit down and I'll make you some chamomile tea. You need — '

'I need something stronger than chamomile tea. I'll have a glass of wine.'

Rose pulled out a chair and sat down at the large old pinewood table. Slumping forward, she put her elbows on the table and propped her chin in her hands. She wondered whether she'd acted too hastily, handing in her notice when her sister and brother-in-law had been killed and she'd suddenly become responsible for Pippa.

After all, she needed to be earning. Hannah and Richard hadn't taken out accidental death policies; like many people, it was one of those things they'd always meant to do but hadn't got around to. Eventually there might be some sort of compensation, but that could be years away. There would be the money from Richard's business when it was sold, but that would be needed for a deposit on the house.

Just before the tragedy, Richard had secured a large order for the ortho-paedic chair he'd designed and had out on trial. That's when he and Hannah had decided to move from the small rented cottage close to Lucy's house into the farmhouse 'over the border in the next county'. They'd negotiated a six-month lease, with the agreement that they'd then buy the property using the remuneration from the order as a deposit. Of course, the order couldn't now be fulfilled.

I could have gone part-time or arranged a job-share and looked for a bigger flat where there was room for Pippa, Rose worried — or even a small house with a garden. But that would have meant staying in the rough, inner-city area and she didn't want that for her niece.

Besides . . . her thoughts spun on and on, and her head began to ache.

Surreptitiously watching her god-daughter whilst opening the wine and observing the bleakness in her expressive grey eyes, Lucy's heart went out to the woman whose parents had been her own closest friends.

One tragedy was bad enough for anyone to cope with. But two . . . and then Rose ending her relationship with Stephen because he was against her taking on the responsibility of Pippa . . .

Lucy shook her head and walked across to the table.

'I take it it's not a celebratory drink,'

she said, putting two glasses down and breaking into Rose's dismal thoughts.

Rose took a couple of sips of wine, then began to tell Lucy everything that had happened.

'You could always come and work at 'Alternatively Yours',' Lucy suggested. 'We need a counsellor and it's a foregone conclusion you'll get your diploma — all your pass grades have been excellent.'

Rose sipped her glass of wine then sighed despondently.

'I might have to take you up on that,' she said quietly. 'But it would be going against my principles to — '

'Rose!' interrupted her godmother. 'You've got to be realistic, love. I know you feel that people shouldn't have to pay for counselling. I know you want to use your skills, your training, as part of your everyday working life but . . . '

'I know what you're going to say and you're right. I haven't actually got an everyday working life — nor the prospects of one after today's fiasco.'

'I wasn't going to say that at all,' protested Lucy. 'I still think you're being too pessimistic about that. From what you said, the other doctors had questioned you quite closely before Dr Knight arrived.'

'So?' said Rose.

'So they wouldn't have bothered to do that if they weren't interested. And as for the episode with little Rosie . . . that showed a sense of responsibility and caring on your part. Good attributes in a person, I reckon.'

'I'm not sure Dr Knight would agree with you, Lucy.'

'It's unlikely he'll hold it against you, Rose. As for your response to the other two doctors, about working part-time, I reckon such a definite reply should work in your favour.'

'Huh! I wish.'

Lucy shook her head. Her god-daughter was clearly in a negative frame of mind.

'What I was going to say was that if you came to work at 'Alternatively

Yours', you could always contact some of the local doctors and let them know you'd be willing to do a counselling clinic for them. You could do some voluntary work. We all do, you know.'

'No, I didn't know. That's terrific, Lucy.'

'Yes, well, it's as well to have a plan of action in case you're right,' Lucy said gently. 'But wait and see.'

'Thanks, Lucy,' said Rose. 'I'll think about it. But for now we'd better start thinking about getting the meal ready. They'll be here soon.'

'We'll need plenty of vegetables,' said Lucy. 'I think Abigail is eating for three, not two.'

'Wishful thinking, Luce,' said Rose. 'You just want to be grandmother to twins.'

The telephone rang just then and Lucy hurried away to answer it. Left on her own, Rose went to the fridge to start preparing the food.

As she grated cheese, she mulled over her godmother's suggestion. Disliking

for a rest, Pippa followed her in and Abigail heard her talking about the crash. She told Topsy that when she'd been coming home in the car with her mummy and daddy from a day out she'd distracted her mummy by laughing and her mummy had crashed the car.'

'That never came out in her sessions with the hospital counsellor,' said Rose. She shook her head. 'I told her . . . I explained that the driver of the coach . . . well, I can't remember exactly how I explained that he'd had a heart attack and lost control, but . . .

'Oh, heck, what am I going to do, Lucy? If I don't do something the guilt will destroy her. And how is Pippa now? Is she upset?'

'No. Well, Abigail says she thinks Pippa is limping very slightly, which might be a sign of stress or might be because she's been running around. But the only comment Pippa made when she came out of the barn was, 'I do hope Auntie Rose will let me have Topsy, too'.'

'Well, if Topsy's the one Pippa has decided to open her heart to, to talk over her secret feelings with, of course we'll have her as well,' said Rose.

She slid off the stool, walked to the sink and filled the kettle.

'I'm making coffee,' she said. 'Thank heavens I only had one small glass of wine. I know it'll mean a late bedtime but I'll take Pippa back to the flat tonight instead of us sleeping here. She'll see it as a chance to ask me about having Topsy and I'll turn it into a chance to see if I can get her to talk about the accident.

'It's a blessing Pippa didn't take against car journeys,' she added, reaching into a cupboard for a jar of coffee. 'I expected her to, you know — I still expect her to at some point, actually. That's why . . . '

'Rose! Stop it,' Lucy said sharply. 'You aren't going anywhere. Well, you are, but you're not driving — and you're certainly not spending time alone.'

Rose spun round. 'What's that supposed to mean?'

The belligerent but forceful reply made Lucy smile. 'That's better.' She stepped forward to envelop Rose in a hug. 'Now listen,' she commanded. 'Abigail suggested that Thomas drops her off here, then he'll take you and Pippa back to the Animal Rescue. You can wander round with Pippa while he examines the new arrivals and interviews a couple of people who want to give a home to some of the animals. It'll give you a chance to watch Pippa on neutral territory, so to speak, and to see if you think she needs another appointment with the hospital counsellor.'

'I know what you're getting at,' Rose said seriously. 'Don't worry, Lucy, I wouldn't jeopardise Pippa's chances of recovery from trauma by trying to handle things on my own.'

'I worry about you as much as Pippa,' Lucy said huskily. 'You haven't been able to take time to grieve yourself, love; haven't had any professional help.'

'I am grieving, though.' Rose leaned back against the sink. 'It really, really hurt when I first heard Dr Knight's niece's name,' she recalled. 'Hannah used to call me Rosie sometimes. She was the only one who did. I mean, I knew it couldn't be her, but . . . ' She blinked hard. 'And you're wrong, Lucy. I saw the hospital counsellor on my own behalf almost every time I went to visit Pippa. And again last week when I took Pippa back to have her leg checked. In fact, I invited Josh to come and see us when we've moved in.'

'As a counsellor, or . . . ?' teased Lucy, trying to ease the atmosphere.

'You'll know the answer to that when you meet him,' Rose teased back. 'If he's off-duty he's coming to help with the move.

'I'll go and do something with my face.' She glanced down at her clothes. 'Can I borrow some jeans and a top? I don't have anything suitable for walking round the animal centre. I've only got what I'm wearing and another respectable outfit for tomorrow. I've arranged with the headmistress of Pippa's new school for us to go in tomorrow to see around. We're going in after morning assembly and Pippa will stay until lunch-time.'

'Of course.' Lucy smiled. 'Help yourself — good job we're about the same size.'

Rose had just finished changing into her borrowed clothes when Abigail hurried into the bedroom.

'OK, Rose?' she asked, walking over to give her a hug. 'I hope I did the right thing, phoning to say what had happened. I had to talk quickly while Pippa was out of the way. That's why I didn't get Mum to call you to the phone.'

'Of course you did the right thing,' Rose told her best friend. 'I'm just glad you happened to overhear Pippa talking. Where is she, Abigail? Is she all right?'

'Waiting in the car. She seems fine. It worked like a charm when I told her I felt a bit tired so Thomas was bringing me here, and then they'd go back. She said you'd probably be here by now, and would like to go with them. So I said I'd run in and see.'

'I didn't know you could be so crafty!' Rose laughed. 'It's good that Pippa thinks it's her idea to take me.'

'Have a good time.' Abigail smiled as Rose dashed away, anxious to see for herself that her niece was all right.

★ ★ ★

When Thomas turned into the parking area outside the Animal Rescue Centre, Rose stared in dismay as she noticed a metallic green Range Rover parked alongside three other cars.

It doesn't have to be his, she told herself. It isn't exactly an uncommon vehicle; plenty of people drive a Range Rover. But . . .

'Are there any puppies here at the

moment, Thomas?' she asked her friend's husband. 'Ones ready to leave?'

'There are, as it happens. Donna, a rough collie, was left on the doorstep a couple of months or so ago with a litter of five. But surely, you're not thinking . . . ?'

'Oh, no. No puppies for us,' she assured him. 'We've agreed on that, haven't we, Pippa?' She twisted round to glance at her niece.

'Yes, we have. It wouldn't be fair to have a dog when we'll both be out every day. I don't mind as long as I can have some chickens and Grizelda. That's the goat I've chosen, Auntie Rose. And . . . ' Pippa's voice faded and she pursed her lips together.

Rose regarded her with scarcely concealed amusement. Much to her relief, she'd detected no sign of disturbance in the little girl's manner during the car ride. Excitement, yes. Pippa adored visiting the animal centre. And now, thought Rose, she was clearly determined not to bring up just yet the subject of having not only Grizelda but her kid as well.

'She'll burst with it soon,' Thomas murmured. Then aloud, 'Well, I'd better get myself inside and examine the new arrivals. One parrot and one pig, would you believe? And I've a couple of people to see who are interested in giving homes to some of Donna's pups,' he added.

It was sounding more and more likely. Rose stared across at the green Range Rover . . .

'Hurry up, Auntie Rose!' Pippa demanded and, smiling an apology, Rose opened the car door and reached in to unfasten her niece's seat-belt.

'I'm going down to the kennels,' Pippa said, the second she was out of the car. 'It's feeding time and James will let me help. You can go and see Grizelda if you like, Auntie Rose. She's in that barn over there. There's a baby goat, too,' she added.

'So that's the way she's playing it,' Rose said dryly, chuckling as Pippa hurried away. 'She's hoping I'll fall in love with Topsy.'

'No sign of her leg playing up,' said Thomas, lifting out his vet's case. 'You coming in with me, Rose, or doing as Pippa suggested?'

'Oh, I'll go and see Grizelda and Topsy and find out what I'm letting myself in for,' she replied.

She would have liked to see the parrot and the pig, too, but if Matthew Knight were here he'd be inside waiting for Thomas. And as much as I'd like to see him, to apologise for what happened outside the school, Rose mused, he might think I'm trying to influence him if I do it now. I will apologise — but I'll wait till I've heard about the job first.

★ ★ ★

Rose spent some time with the Saanen and her kid, glad to find that they both seemed fairly placid and friendly, before making her way to the kennel area.

57

As she approached, she heard Pippa say, 'No, I'm not here to choose a puppy. I've been helping James feed them. I come here quite often with Thomas. He's my godfather and he's a vet and he looks after all the animals here. I'm having a goat when we move to Morden.'

'My uncle's waiting to see the vet 'cos we . . . I'm here to choose a puppy.'

Recognising Rosie's voice, Rose breathed a sigh of relief. She'd been right not to go inside with Thomas. She could see the house and the outbuildings from where she was standing. No sign of anyone — she'd keep a watch and make herself scarce if Dr Knight appeared.

'I think I'll have this one,' Rosie continued. 'It was the first one to come to me. Do you like it?'

'I like them all,' replied Pippa. 'But I like their mummy best. She's called Donna and James is having her when they've found homes for all her puppies.'

'She's like Lassie, isn't she? But the puppies don't look like Lassie.'

'They might when they get bigger. I think the one you like is going to be very big.'

Rose smiled as she listened to and watched the two little girls who were kneeling on the ground surrounded by puppies.

'I'm going to call it Here-Boy,' Rosie announced positively. 'Here-Boy, Here-Boy. See — it's come to me!'

Pippa picked up the puppy and turned it on its back. 'You can't call it that,' she scoffed.

'Why can't I? Anyway, it's not up to you. It's my puppy.'

'It's a bitch.'

'Ooh. That's a naughty word!'

'Not when you're talking about dogs it isn't. And this is a bitch. A girl dog. Look it hasn't got a . . . you know.'

Rose was shaking with silent laughter.

'Uncle Matt said I couldn't have a girl dog,' said Rosie dolefully. 'But maybe he won't notice she hasn't got one.'

This was Rose's undoing. Overcome by mirth she stepped back, bent double . . . and bumped into someone behind her, someone who was laughing as hard as she was. The two of them staggered, their combined weights causing them to fall, domino-like, to the ground.

'Oh, good grief,' muttered a voice. 'That's the funniest thing I've ever . . . '

Rose found herself almost sitting on the lap of someone who was laughing even harder than she was.

'I'm sorry, Miss Winter,' Rose felt his breath warm against the back of her neck. 'Are you all right?' he managed to gasp.

'Uncle Matt! Auntie Rose!' Two shocked voices came in unison before Rose could either move or reply. Then, like a shot from a cannon, Pippa appeared.

'What are you doing to my Auntie Rose? Let go of her! She's crying. You've hurt her.'

Getting no response except helpless groans from both of them, Pippa grabbed Dr Knight's hair and started to pull.

Rosie, seeing her uncle under attack, tried to pull Pippa away. The puppies decided to join them and Donna barked her encouragement.

James and Thomas arrived just then and scooped up the puppies, staring in amazement at the two adults — now kneeling face to face and clasping each other's arms for support — and the two very angry little girls.

Eventually Rose managed to scramble to her feet, but she was powerless to prevent Pippa from hurling herself at Dr Knight. He would have managed to hold her off if Rosie hadn't hurled herself at Pippa. As it was, he ended up flat on his back with both little girls on top of him.

Rose just stood there, her eyes fastened on his lean, muscular body as he tussled playfully with the giggling children.

'Don't just stand there!' Matthew Knight protested. 'Someone get these two ruffians off me!'

But Rose couldn't make herself move.

James and Thomas glanced at her then moved swiftly to the kennel enclosure, popped the pups inside, closed the wire-netting door, and turned back to each pull a wriggling child off Matthew Knight.

As he got up, his eyes unerringly found Rose's. 'I see your niece is like you for jumping to conclusions,' he said, but the laughter was still in his voice and his eyes sparkled with amusement.

'Seems to be well up on anatomy, too,' he added with a broad smile.

'She . . . er . . . she spends quite a lot of time on Thomas and Abigail's smallholding,' Rose began to explain.

'What's an . . . an-a-to-my?' Pippa interrupted.

'Don't get her going again, Rose, please,' begged Dr Knight.

'Er . . . do you and Dr Knight know

62

each other then, Rose?' Thomas asked
with some bewilderment.

Rose couldn't answer; she was too
busy thinking how Matthew Knight had
called her 'Rose', of the warm feeling it
had brought, of the way his dark eyes
crinkled when he laughed . . .

'I know her,' said Rosie, suddenly
recognising Rose. 'She cuddled me
when I was crying. And that's what
Uncle Matt was doing,' she added,
looking at Pippa. 'He was cuddling her
'cos she was crying.'

'That's all right then,' said Pippa.
'Let's go and look at the puppies again.
My name's Pippa. What's yours?'

'Is someone going to explain?'
Thomas asked plaintively as, hand in
hand and chattering nineteen to the
dozen, Pippa and Rosie went back into
the enclosure.

Rose looked towards Matthew
Knight again. Their eyes locked and
held; the spark of electricity flowing
between them almost a tangible thing.

'Thomas. We want you,' called Pippa,

breaking the spell. 'See, Rosie wants this puppy, but her uncle doesn't want the 'sponsibility of lots of litters of puppies.'

'No, Pippa. It was Aunt Pamela who said that, not Uncle Matt . . .'

The rest of Rosie's words were lost on Rose. Aunt Pamela . . . Rosie's aunt, Matt's wife. Rose closed her eyes against the pain that thought brought. And she was even thinking of him as Matt, she despaired.

'I'll leave you to sort things out, Dr Knight,' she managed, praying that he didn't notice her croaky voice. Then, turning away from him she called, 'Thomas, I'm going to have another look at the goats. I'll wait in the barn for you and Pippa.'

Rose knew she was being watched as she walked away; the tingling awareness running down her back told her that. She forced herself not to look round, scared of what she might feel if, even from a distance, she met Matthew Knight's deep brown gaze.

'You don't fancy giving her this, do you?' a harassed-looking girl, holding a feeding bottle, walked up to Rose as she knelt stroking the small kid. 'I've got a problem with one of the goats outside and I need to get to her.'

'Sure — it'll be good practice,' said Rose, standing up and taking the bottle. 'My niece has set her heart on having this little one as well as Grizelda.'

'She'll play you up at first,' the girl warned. 'But once you've got her sucking she should be fine,' she added as she hurried away.

'OK, Topsy,' Rose murmured, 'let's see what we can do.'

Every time Rose got the feeding bottle near the kid it pushed it away. 'Right,' said Rose, when a few more attempts had failed, 'we'll try it this way.' She squeezed the teat, squirted some milk on to her fingers and rubbed them around the kid's mouth. It sniffed then started licking. Gently Rose moved her fingers to make the kid's mouth open, then she pushed the teat in.

'See?' she said, watching it suck. 'You wanted it really, didn't you? When you come to live with us, I'm going to rub some flower remedy behind your ears before feeding time to calm you down.'

Leaning against the doorframe, Matthew watched as Rose encouraged the kid to keep sucking. He guessed Rose hadn't heard him come into the barn. He tried telling himself he hadn't alerted her to his presence because he didn't want to startle her. But he knew he was lying. It was a pleasure to watch her; she was so gentle, so patient, and so feminine.

He felt a tugging at his heartstrings as she stroked one of the kid's ears. That feeling is guilt because you treated her so harshly outside the school and you gave her a hard time at the interview. And because you hadn't read her letter properly, he insisted silently.

Pull yourself together — you came to find her to tell her something, so get over there and tell her.

Rose was suddenly aware of a tingling at the back of her neck. She looked over her shoulder to see Matthew walking towards her — and looked quickly back at the kid as she felt her face turning warm.

'Where are the girls?' she asked for something to say.

'Your friend Thomas is giving Rosie some puppy-rearing hints,' he replied. 'Pippa said she'd stay in case he forgot anything.'

'That sounds like Pippa.' Rose concentrated on tilting the feeding bottle to make sure Topsy didn't suck in any air.

'Our nieces have certainly taken a liking to each other,' he added.

'It amazes me how quickly children make friends,' Rose mumbled. She couldn't bring herself to look at him — he was disturbing her equilibrium enough already. As she tugged the now empty feeding bottle from the kid's mouth, she wondered how long they could keep up this stilted conversation.

What's he doing here anyway? she thought as she watched the kid skip away to join its mother at the hay net.

'I came to apologise,' he said, as though he'd read her thoughts.

'Apologise?' She looked at him and her heart beat faster as she met his gaze.

'About what happened outside the school. I was angry with you when really I should have been thanking you for your concern.' He ran one hand around the neck of his sweatshirt, looking uncomfortable. Wanting to put him at ease, Rose reached up and touched his arm.

'You weren't angry. You were upset,' she corrected.

'Yes . . . well . . . ' He took a hasty step back and Rose quickly lowered her hand and began to fiddle with the feeding bottle.

'Then at the interview,' he went on, 'I

was rather harsh. If I'd read your letter properly . . . if I'd known you were caring for your niece, and about your family bereavement . . . I wouldn't have asked if you intended to take up private counselling in your spare time.'

'That's OK, forget it. And now . . . ' Rose, anxious to put some space between them, searched her mind for an excuse to leave, ' . . . I'd better go and tell someone that Topsy finished all her milk. They'll want to make a note of it.'

'Wait!' he caught her arm as she turned away. 'As well as coming to apologise, I came to tell you that the job is yours. That's if you still want it after we gave you such a tough time,' he added with a wry smile.

He was still holding her arm; his touch, his closeness was making her senses whirl. Rose was furious with herself. He was married, for heaven's sake. She shouldn't be feeling like this. Like what? It's sympathy because we're in a similar position, that's all.

'My partners and I feel you have a great deal to offer our practice,' he was saying. 'But you needn't give me your decision now — you obviously need time to think about it. You'll be getting an official letter in a couple of days and you can reply in writing. I only told you because you happened to be here and I thought you'd like to know.'

'I don't need time to think about it,' Rose told him. 'I — '

Before she had time to say any more, Pippa and Rosie dashed into the barn.

'Auntie Rose, is the school I'll be going to called Morden Primary?' asked Pippa. ''Cos that's where Rosie goes. She's five and we're best friends now and that's the school I want to go to.

'Have you been feeding Topsy? Do you like her? Grizelda's her mummy, you know, and we're having Grizelda aren't we and I . . . '

'Stop!' Rose laughed and ruffled her hair. 'Fizzle down, Pippa. Give me a chance to answer one question at a time, hmm? The answers are yes, you'll be going to Morden Primary, yes I've been feeding Topsy, yes, I like her, yes, we are having Grizelda and . . . and yes, we'll have Topsy as well,' said Rose.

'How did you know I was going to ask that?' demanded Pippa. 'Oh, isn't it great, Rosie? You can share my goats and I can share your puppy. And now you've got to ask your uncle your question. He's a doctor, you know,' she added turning back to Rose.

'I know he is,' Rose replied. 'And,' she continued, 'next week I'll be working with him and the other doctors at the health centre.'

'That's good,' said Pippa.

'Yes it is.' Matthew acknowledged Rose's decision with a terse nod. Inwardly he was berating himself for comparing the way Rose acted with Pippa to the much cooler way Pamela acted with Rosie.

Rosie tugged at his hand and he looked down at her. 'What's the question then, poppet? We're only having one puppy,' he added hastily.

'I only want one,' said Rosie. 'As long as it's the girl one. I'm not calling it Here-Boy; I'm calling it Sasha. James is getting her ready now, then you'll have to sign some papers and we can take her home.'

'She wants to know if she can come to the out-of-school club with me,' said Pippa.

Matthew looked questioningly at Rose and she gave him a brief run-down on what and where it was.

'You won't have to take her there,' said Pippa. 'They come to fetch us from school in a mini-bus. You'll have to come and get her though.'

'Can I? Can I go, Uncle Matt?' asked Rosie. 'I'd still be able to look after Sasha and do puppy-training things with her.'

'We'll talk it over with Aunt Pamela when we get home,' Matthew replied. 'And if we don't get home soon, she'll be wondering where we are.'

'I'll see you when you come to school, Pippa,' said Rosie, skipping towards the barn door.

'And I'll see you next week, Miss Winter,' said Matthew. 'I do hope taking on two goats won't interfere with your working hours.'

'It won't, Dr Knight. Just as you won't let taking on a puppy interfere with your work,' Rose retorted.

He gave her a grin and hurried off after his niece.

'You can have a few minutes to say goodbye to Grizelda and Topsy, then we'll go and find Thomas,' Rose told Pippa. She knew Pippa would stretch out saying her goodbyes, which would give Matthew Knight time to get away.

Rose didn't want to see any more of him today. Next time they met would be at the health centre, things would be on a purely professional footing and there would be no hidden undercurrents.

Even so, she hoped they wouldn't be thrown together too much at work.

First Day At Work

Rose parked her car in one of the staff spaces and switched off the ignition. Although there were already quite a lot of cars parked in the main area, she was twenty minutes early, which gave her time to compose herself. She had butterflies in her stomach, a mixture of excitement and apprehension; she'd forgotten how it felt to be starting a new job.

When she'd received her letter, it had contained a breakdown of her working hours and the times of the special clinics she would be helping to run. There had also been a hand-written postscript suggesting she might like to call in and take a 'guided tour'. She'd done that on the Friday. Although she hadn't seen any of the doctors, she'd spent some time with the two other practice nurses who were both senior to her. She knew she'd be happy working alongside either Shirley or Julia.

But there had been so much to do over the weekend, even though she'd had plenty of help. Josh, Pippa's counsellor, had kept his word and come to help with the move. Rose mentioned to Josh how Abigail had overheard Pippa blaming herself for her parents' accident. He'd found an opportune moment to have a few quiet words with the little girl, and as she'd snuggled down in bed on the first night in her new bedroom, Pippa had said sleepily that she'd stopped thinking the accident was her fault.

On the Sunday, they'd explored the area around the farmhouse, then had an impromptu barbecue in the garden. So, all in all, she hadn't had time to think about her new job.

Yesterday, whilst unpacking the last of the boxes, all her thoughts had been for Pippa on her first full day at her new school. But she needn't have worried; Pippa loved her school and had been impatient to get there this morning.

Rose smiled as she recalled her niece's words: 'You don't have to come in to school with me this morning. The lollipop lady can take me across the road. You can get to work early and have a sit down and a nice cup of tea before you start taking blood out of people's arms and listening to hearts and stuff.'

Still smiling, Rose got out of the car. She glanced at the metallic green vehicle parked at the far end of the staff area and was glad to feel no reaction.

It was a welcoming car park, she thought, as she made her way past the cars in the main area. Trees and bushes along two sides and flower-baskets full of winter pansies hanging from the lamp-posts . . .

'Whoops!' She laughed as a little girl of about Pippa's age almost ran into her.

'You're a nurse, aren't you?' the child asked. 'You've got nurse's clothes on and you work in there.' She waved a hand towards the building. 'What's your name?'

Rose didn't know how informal the other practice nurses were but she liked children especially to feel they could relate to her.

'I'm Nurse Rose,' she replied.

'Mummy's brought me here 'cos of my itchy arm. Will you look at it? I'll take my anorak off and show you.'

'Samantha! I told you to stand by the car while I got the baby out.' A grown-up version of Samantha hurried up to them. She sighed and smiled ruefully at Rose. 'I need eyes in the back of my head.' She turned back to the child, 'Sam, just wait until we get inside before you start undressing yourself.'

'But I want to — '

'No, just listen, Sam — I've got to get Daniel's car cot unstrapped and I want you to wait by the car until I've done it. Now come on. You can show Nurse your rash when it's our turn to see her.'

For a split second, Rose thought the

desperate sobbing that reached her ears came from Samantha as her mother hustled her away. Then she realised it was coming from inside the car parked to her right.

A woman was crouched forward over the steering wheel. All Rose could see was a mass of curly red hair and the white clenched hands the woman's face was buried in. And now there was the thin wailing of a young baby, too.

Rose stepped quickly to the passenger side of the car and tried the door. It opened and, leaning inside, Rose glanced across at the baby in the car cot on the back seat. Then she gently touched the woman's arm. 'I'm one of the practice nurses. Can I help?' she asked.

The woman lifted a tear-stained face. 'No-one can help. The health visitor and the doctors keep telling me I've got a nice healthy baby. Dr Gordon has just checked him over and can't find anything wrong with him. So why does he keep crying like that?'

Rose glanced across at the baby again and smiled. He had red curls just like his mum. 'He's dropping off to sleep now,' she said. 'Shall I get in and sit with you a while?'

The woman straightened up. 'If you like,' she replied dully.

Rose got into the car. 'I'm Rose,' she said, as she closed the door.

'I'm Penny,' said the young mother.

'And what's the baby's name?'

'Adam. Adam the Angry, my husband calls him.' said Penny, scrubbing at her face. 'Heavens, I must look a mess,' she added.

Rose shook her head. 'Just a bit tired,' she said. 'Now tell me about Adam. Go through a usual day with me — when you bath him, how often you feed him, where you sit when you feed him, when you take him out in his buggy, things like that.'

Penny started talking, haltingly and in a voice that broke more than once. Every time the tension lines in the young woman's face deepened, Rose quietly interrupted with a question or a suggestion.

Ten minutes later, Penny was actually smiling and anxious to get home to put some of Rose's ideas to the test.

'I'll come to the baby clinic on Thursday to tell you how we're getting on,' she said. 'Thank you for sparing the time to listen.'

'That's all right,' Rose replied. 'I had time to spare. I was early.'

Was being the operative word, Rose thought as she hurried towards the entrance. Now she was late.

★ ★ ★

'Just arrived, Nurse Winter? Not exactly an auspicious start.'

She was on the way to her treatment room, coat over her arm and clutching a small pile of buff folders and her patient list. Why the heck did it have to be Dr Knight walking up the corridor towards her?

'Sorry, I — '

'It's hard enough for any of us to see patients at the time they're booked in for,' Matthew cut across her words. 'The whole point of us taking on an extra practice nurse was to try to alleviate the problem, not to add to it.'

He looks tired and stressed, thought Rose, observing the tension lines around his mouth, the shadows under his eyes — and the shadows *in* his eyes, too. I wonder if . . .

'You were due at nine-fifteen,' Matthew continued. 'When my partners and I worked out how we should break down your hours, I suggested that time rather than nine o'clock to give you time to see your niece into school first. I do hope you aren't one of those people who're always late.'

In spite of his harsh — even arrogant — attitude, she wanted to smooth away the deep lines on his face, get rid of the haunted look in his brown eyes.

Annoyed with herself she answered crossly: 'Well, now I am here, Dr Knight, perhaps you'll let me get started on my patient list?'

Before he could comment, a child's voice rang out: 'But I don't *want* to see this nurse — I want to see Nurse Rose.'

The senior practice nurse appeared at the other end of the corridor with the child and mother who had spoken to Rose in the car park.

'There she is, see?' The little girl tugged her hand away from her mother's and ran down the corridor to Rose. 'I want you to look at it. You said you would, Nurse Rose. When I was talking to you outside, you said you would.'

'Did you?' murmured Matthew.

Rose shook her head before crouching down in front of the child. 'Samantha, your name isn't on my list of people I've got to see today. Perhaps next time you come you can — '

'No. No. I want *you* to look at it.'

'Nurse Winter, why don't you give me the notes of your first patient?' Julia Chadwick suggested. 'I'll see them and you can see Samantha. If that's all right with you, Mrs Webster?' she added, looking at Samantha's mother.

'It's fine,' Mrs Webster replied. 'But I am sorry about this. I . . . '

Rose smiled. 'That's sorted then. I'll take Samantha through to my room now.'

'I'll fetch Samantha's folder for you, Nurse Winter,' said Julia.

'No need, I'll get it.' Matthew walked off towards Julia's treatment room.

To Rose's amazement, when Matthew came into her treatment room with the folder, he closed the door behind him.

'I'm on roving duty this morning,' he said. 'I might as well stay and see if you're going to need me to sign a prescription. That is, if nobody minds?'

Rose guessed his last words were aimed at her. But she smiled down at Samantha and said, 'We don't mind if he stays with us, do we?'

Samantha shook her head. 'But I don't want him to look at my rash. I want *you* to.'

'OK,' said Rose. 'Your mum can sit on that chair.' Rose indicated a chair. 'You sit on this one, Samantha, and roll your sleeve up while I wash my hands and get my treatment tray.'

That done, she crouched down by Samantha's chair.

Matthew sat on the office chair and watched her. She had a knack with children — they responded to her. Even his own niece, who hadn't seen Rose since last week at the Animal Rescue Centre, had mentioned Pippa's auntie almost every day. And this morning, when Rosie had been upset, she'd said she wished she could have Pippa's auntie instead of Aunt Pamela.

Which is probably why I was so annoyed when I saw Rose hurrying because she was late. It wasn't because I found myself fascinated by her bright eyes and flushed cheeks, it's because Rosie keeps talking about her, comparing her unfavourably to Pamela.

'Did Samantha have eczema when she was younger?' Rose was asking Mrs

Webster as she looked at the cracked and scaly skin in the crease of Samantha's elbow.

Mrs Webster sighed. 'Yes. I thought it might be starting up again.'

'It itches,' said Samantha. 'And it stings when I scratch it. Is it the ex-thingie come back?'

'I think it might be eczema,' Rose replied. 'You're going to have to try very hard not to scratch it, Samantha. We'll have to think of something to stop it itching. How about letting the doctor have a look at your arm, and we'll see what he thinks?'

'He won't frown at me like he was frowning at you, will he?' Samantha asked in a loud whisper.

'I think Dr Matthew was frowning because he had a headache,' Rose whispered back, her eyes meeting Matthew's over the child's head. 'He's smiling now, sweetheart, so I guess his headache has gone.'

'OK, he can look.'

Samantha slid off her chair and went

across to Matthew.

'Nurse Winter . . . er, Nurse Rose is right. It is eczema, Samantha. I'll give your mum some cream she can put on it for you.'

'Will it hurt?' Samantha asked.

'It might make your arm tingle just a little bit,' he replied. 'But I'll see if I can think of some magic words so it won't hurt too much. Do you want to watch while I make the computer print out a prescription?'

Matthew swung round to the computer and tapped away at the keyboard.

'Do you think the eczema has been brought on because of her new baby brother?' Mrs Webster asked Rose quietly, looking down at the baby asleep in his car cot. 'She doesn't seem to be jealous of him. I make sure to pay her extra attention at his feeding times. I let her help get things ready and I give her a glass of milk and read her a story while I'm feeding him.'

'So she's drinking more milk than she used to?' asked Rose.

'Yes. Could that be it?' Mrs Webster looked concerned.

'You could maybe try — '

'In the past, goat's milk was often suggested as an alternative to cow's milk,' Matthew interrupted. 'However, recent reports have shown that a reaction to goat's milk can also develop.'

'I was going to suggest trying soya milk for a while.' Rose spoke quietly but Matthew noticed the steely glint in her grey eyes as she looked at him.

'Yes, that's a good idea,' he agreed.

'And although drinking goat's milk might not be advisable,' said Rose, 'a goat's milk soap can often help.'

'I'll try both ideas as well as using the cream on her and taking all the usual precautions.' Mrs Webster lifted the car cot and stood up. 'Come on, Samantha, we've taken up enough of Nurse Rose's and Dr Knight's time.'

'Nurse Rose said he was called Dr Matthew,' Samantha pointed out.

'Ah, I only let very special people call

me that,' Matthew said, walking over to open the door.

Rose's heart lurched at his words. But that was silly. Matthew was referring to Samantha — not to her.

'Daniel is due for his jabs in a couple of weeks,' Mrs Webster said as she ushered Samantha out. 'So I'll see you then.'

'Come back before that if Samantha's rash isn't getting any better,' Matthew said before closing the door.

Rose reached out for the next patient's file. 'Mrs Bennett for a blood pressure test,' she murmured.

'Well, you should be able to do that quickly enough,' Matthew said tersely. 'You might be able to make up a bit of time. And don't forget the lunchtime meeting.'

Before Rose could reply, he'd opened the door and gone.

'Talk about Jekyll and Hyde,' she muttered furiously.

The rest of the morning passed quickly. Rose took blood samples, syringed ears and changed dressings, and her last patient of the morning was an anaemic woman who needed a course of iron tablets.

And that leaves me with a couple of minutes to tidy myself before going to the staff room, Rose thought, when she'd seen the woman out.

She had just picked up her handbag when her phone rang. It was Linda. 'I hoped I'd catch you before the meeting,' said the receptionist. 'Julia isn't answering her phone, she must be on her way to the staff room. I've got a little lad here with a splinter in his bottom.'

'OK, I'll see him,' said Rose.

'You'll have to come to Reception. His grandmother is with him. She brings him so often she should know her way round the place better than I do, but she doesn't speak much English.'

'On my way,' said Rose. 'And thanks for the warning!'

It took Rose fifteen minutes to calm

down the little boy and remove the splinter. Luckily she didn't have to ask the grandmother about a tetanus injection; his records showed his vaccinations were up to date. She gave him a sweet for being so brave, then walked down the corridor with him and his grandmother.

'And now I'm late for the second time today,' Rose muttered as she hurried to the staff room.

★ ★ ★

'Ah, Nurse, did something keep you?' Matthew asked as she walked in. He was standing by a small table, pouring a cup of coffee.

'Don't tease her, Matthew,' said Audrey Gordon. She smiled across at Rose. 'Grab a drink then make yourself comfortable, Rose. Linda told us she'd landed you with Tariq and his grandmother,' she continued. 'What was it this time?'

'A nasty splinter in his bottom,' Rose

the idea of people having to pay for counselling wasn't her only reason for not wanting to work with the therapists who, a couple of years ago, had joined together to set up 'Alternatively Yours'.

Her other reason was her four-and-a-half-year-old niece. Rose wasn't sure whether Pippa would be able to accept the idea.

It might upset her if I were to work where Hannah had worked, acknowledged Rose. Even though I wouldn't be taking Hannah's place as a reflexologist, Pippa would see it as a sort of trespass.

'What do you think, Marmaduke?' she murmured. She glanced at Lucy's cat who had leapt up onto a stool and was watching her every move. 'Pippa seems happy enough at the thought of going to the 'out of school club' even though it's in the same building as the play-group she went to when Hannah was working. It's not quite the same as it was before. She'll be with the older children and with different staff.

When I collect her, I won't be collecting her from the same room as Hannah did.'

Marmaduke mewed plaintively; Rose scooped a few slivers of grated cheese from the bowl and took them to him.

'Oh, it's so hard to work it all out,' she sighed as Marmaduke savoured his tit-bit. 'I wonder if Dr Knight goes through this sort of thing when deciding what's best for Rosie? Is he getting her a puppy for the same reasons I've agreed to letting Pippa have a goat and some chickens? To make her feel needed, giving her a responsibility to help stop her from dwelling on things?'

She rubbed the soft fur between the cat's ears. 'Does he sometimes feel as helpless and as frightened as I do, Marmaduke?'

The cat gazed at her.

'You're right. How did he enter into this?' she demanded. 'He's not the only person I've come across in a similar situation to mine. Why am I wondering replied. 'Thank you,' she said, taking the cup of coffee Matthew offered her before making for the nearest chair.

'You're welcome,' Matthew said with a smile that made her heart beat faster. She was glad when Harry Sinclair cleared his throat and got to his feet.

'This isn't the usual time for a practice meeting,' he said. 'I just thought it would be nice if we got together to welcome our new nurse.' He looked at Rose and held up his mug. 'So, welcome, Rose.'

'Thank you,' replied Rose. 'I'm afraid I didn't get off to a very good start though.'

'You're forgiven. I'm sure you'll do your best to arrive on time in future,' said Matthew.

Rose felt a tide of colour wash across her face and, to hide it, bent down and put her mug of unfinished coffee on the floor.

'Actually, I was talking about snaffling Julia's patient. We only chatted briefly in the car park,' she explained, looking at the other nurse. 'I told her my name, but I didn't tell her I'd look at her arm.'

'No problem,' Julia said easily. 'Samantha obviously took a shine to you.'

'Rose engineered that,' said Matthew.

Rose glared at him. 'What's that supposed to mean?'

'Whoa, steady,' he protested, holding up his hands. 'When you told Samantha your name, what did you call yourself?'

So that's what he's getting at, she thought. Well, if he doesn't approve of 'Nurse Rose', that's tough. Surely the way she wanted to be addressed was up to her?

'I'm guessing you told Samantha you're Nurse Rose, yes?'

Rose compressed her lips and nodded.

She's got tiny dimples at the corners of her mouth, Matthew observed, forgetting for the moment what he'd been about to say.

'Are you trying to make some sort of point, Matt?' Audrey Gordon's amused voice brought him to his senses.

'Yes, I am,' he said. 'I stayed in the treatment room with Rose when she saw Samantha. When Rose wanted me to confirm the rash was eczema, she referred to me as Dr Matthew, and — '

'I'm sorry if you didn't like that,' interrupted Rose. 'But I think a less official title puts children more at ease.'

'That's my point,' Matthew replied. 'I think perhaps it's something we could all adopt when seeing the younger patients.'

'I'll go along with that,' said Julia. 'I must admit I'm not keen on the modern way of encouraging patients to call nurses by their first names. I know it's supposed to make us seem more approachable,' she continued, 'but I'm proud of my title and like it to be used. But I can see that little ones might feel in awe of it. Nurse Julia is a happy compromise. And I'm sure Shirley will agree too — I'll tell her about it when she comes on duty.'

'That's settled then,' said Matthew.

He turned to look at Linda. 'Perhaps you and the other receptionists could refer to us in that way when it's a child who's booked in to see us?'

Linda chuckled. 'OK, Nurse Matthew.

'Anything else anyone wants to discuss?' asked Harry Sinclair.

'I've got a dental appointment on Thursday and might not be back in time for the Mother and Baby clinic,' said Julia. 'And Shirley can't cover for me, she's got a wart clinic.'

'In that case, Rose can assist me,' said Matthew.

'Nothing else?' Harry asked. 'Well, I'd just like you to know that Rose has come up with an interesting suggestion for Bert Jackson's stubborn leg ulcers — one of her complementary medicines.'

'You mean you've actually decided to try it, Harry?' Matthew sounded amazed. His colleague wasn't known for adapting to new ideas.

'Orthodox treatment hasn't helped,'

the older doctor conceded. 'Rose is bringing some in tomorrow. And I've told Bert to come to see me every day for the next week or so, starting tomorrow. Obviously I'll be keeping a strict eye on his progress, since this is something we haven't tried before.'

'And I can assure you, Dr Knight, if at any time I feel the treatment isn't working, I will discontinue it,' Rose said icily.

Matthew looked steadily at her, but made no reply.

Linda stood up and walked towards the door. 'If you'll all excuse me,' she said into the uncomfortable silence, 'I want to do a bit of shopping before we open up again.'

'Me, too,' said Julia, gathering up her empty cup and her handbag.

Audrey Gordon got to her feet as well. 'I've got a pile of paperwork to get through before afternoon surgery,' she said. 'I'll see you later, Rose — we're doing the Well Woman Clinic together.'

'I have some phone calls to make,'

Harry Sinclair said, following Audrey.

Huh! Leaving Matthew and me alone so we can disagree without an audience, Rose thought. Well, I'm not going to be first to speak.

* * *

'So there I was, forcing cold coffee down my throat, waiting to see what he'd say, and he just mumbled something about a house visit and off he went. Leaving me sitting there,' Rose said.

'Feeling?' asked Lucy, handing Rose the bottle of tincture she'd called in for after she'd picked up Pippa from out-of-school club.

'Silly and annoyed,' Rose admitted ruefully. 'I can't make him out. One minute he's approving of something I've done or said, the next he's criticising me — and then he walks away from me without doing either.'

'I think you're over-reacting. You're probably on the defensive with him because of what happened the first time you met.'

Rose nodded thoughtfully. 'You could be right. Anyway, I didn't see him any more after that. My afternoon session was really busy and then I did a clinic with Audrey.'

'So that was a day in the life of Rose Winter.' Lucy laughed.

Rose pointed to Pippa playing in Lucy's garden. 'It isn't finished yet,' she said, knocking on the window to call her niece in. 'If I stay here chattering any longer, instead of getting me and Pippa home,' she added, as the little girl ran in, 'there won't be much of the day left by the time she's had her tea, her bath and her bedtime story.'

'We better get home quickly, Auntie Rose, 'cos I'll have to do my homework, too,' Pippa said importantly. 'I've got to make two seed pictures to take to school tomorrow.'

A Cuddle For Rosie

Rose woke and stretched — then frowned as last night's half-remembered dream floated through her mind: Matthew standing at the door of her treatment room holding a watch . . . Matthew scowling and pointing at the watch then telling her she was late again.

And then what? Something else happened in that dream, I know it did. She closed her eyes again, willing herself to remember. But she couldn't. And she shouldn't. He was a married man, for heaven's sake.

'So why does he haunt me so much?' she muttered. 'It's got to stop. I can't help what I dream, but I can stop thinking about him when I'm awake.'

'Auntie Rose, who are you talking to?'

Rose opened her eyes and turned her head. Pippa was standing by her bed;

she hadn't heard her come into the room.

'I was talking to myself.' Rose chuckled and, rolling over, she reached out to give Pippa a hug. 'Did you sleep well, sweetheart?'

'Yes,' Pippa replied. She gave Rose a kiss then wriggled out of her arms. 'But I'm very awake now and I want to get ready for school. Do you think Miss Marvin will like the seed pictures we made last night? She said if everyone in our class made a picture there would be enough to cover the wall in the hall for the Harvest Festival.'

Pippa skipped towards the bedroom door. 'Can I go and get washed now, Auntie Rose?'

'Wait a minute, Pippa. You told me you had to make two pictures.'

'Well, I did have to. The other one is for Rosie. She said her Aunt Pamela wouldn't let her make one 'cos sticking on seeds was messy and her Aunt Pamela doesn't like doing messy things.'

Pippa looked anxiously at Rose. 'I think Rosie had been crying before she came to school yesterday. And I thought she might cry today if she hadn't got a picture. It was all right making one for her, wasn't it?'

Rose blinked and swallowed. 'It was very all right, Pippa,' she said huskily.

'That's OK, then. Can I go and get washed now?'

While she waited for Pippa to come out of the bathroom, Rose tidied the bedrooms and thought about what her niece had said. Children exaggerated, of course; Pamela Knight couldn't be as unfeeling as Rosie was making her out to be. The little girl was obviously finding it hard to cope with her parents' death and probably Pamela was finding it just as hard to cope with Rosie's grief. Feeling helpless would frustrate Pamela, maybe make her short-tempered.

Perhaps I should invite Rosie and Pamela to tea? Would it help Pamela to talk things over with someone in a similar position? No, I couldn't do that. Matthew might not like it. He might feel I was interfering.

Rose sighed. Here he is again, leaping into my mind. It's got to stop, she told herself again.

Pippa came in then and Rose's thoughts turned back to her. 'OK, Tiddlywink, your clothes are laid out ready for you on that chair. You get dressed and I'll go for my shower and get dressed myself.'

'Why aren't you wearing your uniform?' Pippa asked a few minutes later as they made their way downstairs and into the kitchen.

'Because I haven't got to go to work until twelve o'clock today,' Rose replied. 'When I've dropped you off at school I'm going to come home and clean out the goat sheds. We want them ready for when Grizelda and Topsy arrive.'

'Not the Saturday coming but the one after,' said Pippa. 'How many days is that, Auntie Rose? It's Wednesday, today, so . . . '

'You choose which cereal you want and start eating it,' Rose urged. 'We'll work out how many days it is on the way to school.'

They'd just finished eating when they heard the letterbox flapping and the sound of letters plopping on to the doormat. Pippa scrambled off her chair and dashed into the hall.

'We've got five letters,' she said, bounding back in with them. 'Only I don't think they are letters,' she added excitedly, handing them to Rose. 'I think they're more 'welcome to your new home' cards. Can I open some, Auntie Rose?'

'All right, but we'll just have a quick look to see who they're from and I'll put them up later. Otherwise you'll be late for school.'

Rose dropped Pippa off by the school crossing, then decided to call in at the farm supply wholesaler for some wellington boots. She'd need them for scrubbing out the goat sheds.

Most of the boots she tried on

seemed to have been designed for giants with long legs and huge feet, but at last she found a pair that fitted her. Pippa will approve of them, she thought, as she handed the bright green and yellow patterned boots to the assistant.

On her way out of the building, Rose met one of the patients she'd treated yesterday and stopped to chat for a while. It was nice to be recognised, nice to feel part of the community, Rose thought as she drove homewards. But it's ten o'clock already. I won't have time to do much, especially as I need a cup of coffee first.

As she stood at the sink filling the kettle, something on the worktop caught her eye. Pippa's seed pictures. With the excitement of opening the cards and then having to hurry, they'd forgotten all about them!

Well, that's that, Rose decided — no coffee and no goat sheds. I'll have to take the seed pictures into school.

The first people Rose saw when she

was let into the school were Miss Marvin, Pippa and Rosie. Rosie was crying and Pippa was holding her hand.

Rose dashed forward, holding out the pictures. 'Is this what's wrong?' she asked. 'Is Rosie upset because we forgot these?'

'No, it isn't that, Auntie Rose. Rosie's upset 'cos she can't tell her mummy and daddy about what we're doing for Harvest Festival. And I . . . ' Pippa's lip trembled. 'I asked her why she didn't go to their special memory place like we do when I want to tell Mummy and Daddy something. And . . . and . . . '

'All right, pet,' Miss Marvin interrupted gently. 'Why don't you and Rose go and sit on those chairs by Miss Peplow's office and look at the pictures while I chat to your auntie?'

'No,' said Pippa. 'Now Auntie Rose is here she can tell Rosie about the memory place. And when Rosie's uncle comes to fetch her, Rosie can tell him 'cos he might not know about it. And he'll be here soon 'cos Miss Peplow left a message for him.'

'You go and look at the pictures, sweetheart,' Rose said. 'I'll have a word with Miss Marvin and then come and sit with you both for a few minutes. OK?'

★   ★   ★

As soon as the little girls were out of earshot Miss Marvin said, 'I feel bad about calling Rosie's uncle from his work, but her aunt doesn't drive.' A worried frown creased her forehead. 'Rosie seemed to settle in all right for the first couple of weeks, but since we've started getting ready for Harvest Festival the poor little mite has had quite a few weepy sessions. This one was the worst, though. Rosie was in such a state, and then . . . '

'Then Pippa mentioned the memory place?' asked Rose, glancing across at the two little girls.

'Yes,' said Miss Marvin. 'And I'm afraid that made Rosie worse. She said if there was somewhere like that, her uncle would have told her.'

'And now Pippa wants me to tell Rosie about it.' Rose sighed. 'But I don't think that's something I should do without getting the go-ahead from her uncle.'

'Could you ask him? Would you?' asked Miss Marvin. 'I believe you already know him? The girls tell me you work together.'

Rose frowned. If it was any other child — any other man . . .

'If it's something you think would help Rosie . . . ' Miss Marvin prompted.

Rose pulled herself together. 'All right, I'll have a word with Dr Knight.'

'I'll go and tell Miss Peplow what's happening,' said Miss Marvin. 'She'll probably want you to wait for Dr Knight in her office.' She was making for the head teacher's door, clearly expecting Rose to follow. 'That will mean I can go back to my class,' she continued. 'I've left them with two assistants, but . . . '

As Miss Marvin knocked on the door, Pippa leapt up from her chair and grabbed Rose's hand. 'Auntie Rose,' she said urgently, 'Rosie says she'll feel better if you give her an all-over-everywhere hug like you give me when I feel sad. That's right, isn't it, Rosie?'

'Yes, please,' Rosie whispered.

Pippa pointed to the chair she'd been sitting on. 'You can sit there, Auntie Rose. It's a good job you're not very big, it's only a small chair.'

Before Rose had time to sit down, Miss Marvin came out of the office. 'Miss Peplow says you can go in,' she said. Then she looked down at Rosie. 'Do you still want Pippa to stay with you, Rosie?'

'Yes, I want Pippa and Pippa's auntie,' Rosie replied.

'Right, I'll see you later then, Pippa,' said Miss Marvin. 'Miss Peplow or your auntie will bring you back to the classroom,' she added as she hurried away.

Once in the office, Pippa pointed to

one of the visitor's chairs. 'You can give Rosie a much better all-over-everywhere hug if you're sitting in a big enough chair, can't you, Auntie Rose?'

Rose glanced at the headmistress.

'Go ahead, Miss Winter,' she said. 'Pippa has told me a little about your methods and I'm sure you'll be able to make Rosie feel better.'

Rose sat down and gathered Rosie on to her lap. 'OK, Rosie, first I'll take your shoes off,' she said.

'She can't cuddle Rosie's toes if she's got shoes on,' Pippa explained to Miss Peplow, before turning to her friend. 'Now you bend your knees, Rosie, and snuggle in close to Auntie Rose. I'll show you.'

Pippa put the seed pictures on Miss Peplow's desk, then began to arrange Rosie's limbs to her satisfaction.

'That's right,' she said, stepping back, 'you're all folded up like a bent banana.'

Rosie gave a little giggle and for a moment Rose just held her.

'Go on, Auntie Rose. Start at her feet,' Pippa commanded.

Stroking and squeezing, Rose worked her way up Rosie's legs.

'You'll have to unbend your legs in a minute,' said Pippa. 'It's nearly time for your tummy to get hugged.'

Just as Rose reached Rosie's tummy the office door opened and Miss Shelton, the school secretary, showed Matthew in.

'What on earth . . . Rose . . . Miss . . . Nurse Winter, what are you doing here?'

Both Rose and Miss Peplow opened their mouths to explain but Pippa got in first. 'Rosie was upset 'cos she couldn't tell her mummy and daddy about Harvest Festival things. I said you should take her to the memory place and she didn't know what I meant,' she gabbled. 'Auntie Rose will be able to tell you all about it, but she's got to finish giving Rosie an all-over-everywhere hug first. It's making Rosie feel better.'

'Don't stop, Pippa's Auntie Rose,' said Rosie when Rose's hands stilled. 'It makes me feel all nice inside, Uncle Matt,' she added, looking up at him.

Rose looked up at him, too. He wouldn't meet her eyes. She could see a muscle twitching in his cheek. What emotion was he fighting to control? Anger? Resentment? Despair?

'Go on, Auntie Rose,' said Pippa. 'The best bit comes next,' she continued. 'Auntie Rose will nuzzle round Rosie's neck then Rosie will laugh and she'll feel better.'

'Is this all right with you, Dr Knight?' Rose asked.

He looked at her then — a hard glance, his eyes almost as black as ebony. Cold.

'It seems to be helping,' he said, and his tone was as cold as his eyes.

How did this happen? Rose asked herself. I only came to give Pippa her pictures . . .

She looked back down at Rosie. 'Ready?' she whispered. Then she bent her head and started rubbing her face over the little girl's neck. Rosie giggled and wriggled and waved her shoeless feet in the air.

When Rose stopped nuzzling, Rosie, her little face bright with laughter, her eyes shining and her black curls tousled, slid off her lap.

'I feel better now,' she said. 'You don't have to take me home, Uncle Matt. I'll stay at school.'

'Are you sure, poppet?' Matthew crouched in front of his niece and ran his hands tenderly over her face.

Even though it wasn't for her Matthew's gentle smile did funny things to Rose's insides.

'I'm sure,' said Rosie.

'See, Dr Knight,' said Pippa, her voice shrill. 'It's just like that day at the Animal Rescue when you and Auntie Rose were on the ground and you cuddled Auntie Rose to make her feel better.'

Rose heard Matthew draw in his breath. She couldn't look at him. She couldn't imagine what interpretation Miss Peplow would put on those words. No — she could. And that was the trouble.

Should she explain? Laugh it off? And what about Matthew? Why wasn't he coming to the rescue? His reputation was at stake here.

So is yours, Rose, said a voice in her head. Play it cool, she told herself, and she forced an impassive expression on to her face.

It felt like hours but it was probably only seconds that passed before Miss Peplow stepped forward and picked up Rosie's shoes. 'Let's put these back on, Rosie,' she said, 'then I'll ask Miss Shelton to take you and Pippa back to the classroom.'

'I'll see to her shoes,' Matthew said, his voice sounding strained.

Miss Peplow nodded, walked to her desk and reached for one of the phones. 'Could you come in, please, Miss Shelton?'

So normal, so everyday, like nothing

has happened, thought Rose, fighting the hysterical laughter that threatened to bubble out.

Pippa went to her aunt's side. 'Don't forget to tell Rosie's uncle about the memory place, will you?' she whispered. 'Rosie's forgotten 'bout it for now but I 'spect she'll remember later.'

'I'll see what I can do, Tiddlywink.'

'Ah, Miss Shelton . . . ' Was that a note of relief in the head teacher's voice? ' . . . Pippa and Rosie are ready to go back to their class now,' Miss Peplow continued. 'Will you take them please?'

Pippa and Rosie said cheerful goodbyes and, hand in hand, left the office with Miss Shelton. When they'd gone, Rose was aware of a clock ticking and of Matthew breathing, but those sounds only seemed to add to the silence of the office.

It was a silence again broken by Miss Peplow. 'Pippa has forgotten her pictures. I'll take them to her.'

Rose sighed. Those pictures had a lot to answer for. And what was she supposed to do now? Get up and say goodbye to Matthew as if nothing had happened? She glanced towards him. He'd turned his back to her; it was rigid and straight.

Matthew shoved his clenched fists into his pockets, wondering what on earth was happening to him. He recalled the vision that had met his eyes when Miss Shelton had showed him into the office: his niece snuggled against Rose's body and Rose with her cheeks flushed and her eyes worried — yes, he'd noticed all that with one fleeting glance.

He hadn't dared to meet Rose's eyes. Why? Because I was afraid of what she might read in my eyes — loneliness and the wish that I could snuggle against her, have her soothing hands on my body and be comforted in the same way as Rosie.

He'd been forced to look at her when she'd asked his permission to carry on.

And he'd been unable to take his eyes from her when she'd nuzzled Rosie's neck, making the little girl laugh in a way he hadn't heard for ages.

Should I thank Rose for her help? What is it with her and children anyway? Look how she captivated Samantha yesterday . . .

He spun round. 'You seem to be Saint Nicholas reincarnated. The patron saint of children,' he added as she gazed at him.

'Right now,' she said, 'I'm more worried about being thought of as a Scarlet Woman thanks to Pippa's unfortunate choice of words.'

To her amazement, Matthew threw back his head and laughed.

Rose stared stonily at him for all of five seconds; then she started to giggle helplessly. They were brought to their senses by the sound of the office door clicking firmly and Miss Peplow noisily clearing her throat.

'Well everything seems to be under control for now, Dr Knight,' she said.

'Rosie and Pippa have joined the rest of the class to hang up their harvest pictures. So unless there is anything you would like to discuss . . . ?'

'No, Miss Peplow. Except, of course, to thank you for sending for me. As you say, everything seems to be under control for now. I'm sure Ro . . . Miss Winter and I don't want to take up any more of your time.'

Rose almost leapt out of her chair in her eagerness to be gone. 'I'm sorry I added to the disruption, Miss Peplow,' she said politely.

'Not at all, Miss Winter. I am just glad you happened to be here. Anything that helps a child in distress is certainly not a disruption. And,' she added, as Matthew and Rose moved towards the door, 'I'm also glad that Pippa and Rosie have become such good friends. I'm sure they will be of great help to each other.'

★ ★ ★

116

'I don't know why we were laughing.' Rose kicked a stone across the playground as she and Matthew walked towards the school gates.

Matthew shrugged. 'Anger, embarrassment, who knows? What I'd like to know, Rose, is . . . ' he touched her arm ' . . . what you were doing at the school?'

It was only the lightest of touches — cool and impersonal. So why was her heart reacting as though it had been a lover's caress?

'Don't sound so disapproving, Matthew,' she flared. 'You aren't the only one with a niece attending the school.'

'You hardly have to remind me of that.'

'Pippa didn't realise what she was saying,' Rose protested. 'Or rather, she didn't realise how Miss Peplow would misconstrue . . . '

'I didn't mean that.' Matthew reached over the top of the school gates to pull back the bolt on the outside, opened the gate and stepped aside for

Rose to go through first.

'What, then?' Rose noticed how his sleeves rode up a little as he re-bolted the gate, noticed the dark hairs that shadowed his wrists.

For heaven's sake, she was acting like a school kid with a crush on her teacher . . .

'Where's your car, or did you walk?' he asked.

'I parked in the side street.'

'We'll sit in my car then.' He'd parked right outside the school. 'In case you hadn't noticed,' he added, 'it's raining. I don't relish the idea of getting soaking wet while we're talking, do you?'

She hadn't noticed it was raining, but he didn't wait for a reply. He strode towards the Range Rover and opened the passenger door for her. She watched him walk round the front of the vehicle and tensed when he slid in next to her.

He turned to face her, resting one arm against the steering wheel. She tried not to notice the fresh tangy scent of his aftershave.

'Shouldn't you be getting back to the health centre?' she asked.

'I'm doing house-calls,' he replied. 'Luckily there's nothing urgent, nothing that can't wait for a little while. The memory place Pippa told Rosie about — is it what I think it is?'

'It was Pippa's bereavement counsellor who suggested to me that she might benefit from visiting her parents' grave,' Rose said quietly. 'I don't know if it would help Rosie or not. I only know it seems to help Pippa.' She kept her eyes lowered. 'I wasn't at all sure about it. I had to make sure Pippa understood that she wouldn't see them, except in her mind, in her heart. I explained that we could take flowers and sit and talk about whatever we wanted . . . The thing is, I couldn't bring myself to call it a grave so I called it the memory place.'

'And you say it's helped Pippa?'

Rose nodded. 'I never suggest going, I leave that up to her. After the first time, I told her to let me know whenever she wanted to go again.'

'And did she want to go again?'

'Yes.' Rose looked at him. 'She asks to go when something new happens . . . like moving house or starting school, or when she's worried or sad — or when she's angry with them for leaving her. Sometimes she talks aloud, other times she just stands there, probably talking inside her head.'

'The same feelings, the same emotions that adults go through, in fact,' said Matthew. 'Rosie came to her parents' funeral service,' he continued, 'but not to the cemetery afterwards.'

'I think that part of it probably would have been too traumatic for a five-year-old,' Rose said thoughtfully. 'I didn't have to face that decision — Pippa was in hospital.'

'But you think I should take Rosie to her parents' grave?'

'I think that has to be your decision. But if you decide yes, and you or Rosie need any help, then . . . '

'Your all-over-everywhere hug certainly

helped her. I do hug and cuddle her, you know, Rose.'

'Oh, Matt, I know you do.' Her heart went out to him. She wanted to hug *him*, to hold him close. But it was impossible, sitting in the car, so she put her hand on his thigh — the only part of him she could reach with a comforting touch.

'I just happened to be there when Rosie needed a hug. Pippa had forgotten to take her homework to school, so I took it in for her. When I got there, Miss Marvin was walking through the entrance hall with Pippa and Rosie. And — '

'But it isn't the same for her when I cuddle her,' Matthew continued. He'd covered her hand with his own in a tight grip, his thumb making circular stroking movements over her wrist. Rose felt warm inside. Suddenly they'd become friends.

'I'm not soft and cosy like you are, Rose.' Matthew sighed. 'I think Rosie misses feminine warmth and softness to snuggle into. Pamela can't provide that, either. Bless her, she's as thin as a rake.'

Pamela. His wife. Rose snatched her hand from under his.

Pippa, in all innocence, must have already caused Miss Peplow to doubt Matthew's character and although Rose knew the head teacher wouldn't say anything to anyone, if someone else were to walk past and see them sitting together like this in Matthew's car, in what could look like an intimate situation, Matthew's reputation might well be shot to pieces.

'I'm sure Rosie gets comfort from either of you cuddling her.' Rose twisted round to open the passenger door. 'I'd best be going. I'm on duty at twelve and I've got to go home and get changed.'

'What did I say?' Matthew muttered as he watched her hurry away through the rain.

His mobile rang just then. Shrugging, he picked it up. Time to get on with what he understood: being a doctor.

A Good Friend

Rose hadn't seen Matthew since her abrupt getaway from his car yesterday. But she'd thought about her hasty action in every idle moment since. She'd wondered if she should mention it to Matthew when she saw him — explain that she'd been worried about his reputation, about someone seeing them and putting two and two together and making five.

Mind you, it might not be a good idea to draw Matthew's attention to it. It might make him wonder if it was because she had feelings for him and therefore felt guilty.

It was true that he was tall, dark and handsome, and the lightest touch from him could make her heart beat faster. But what of it? That didn't mean she was actually hankering after him, did it?

In fact, before he'd brought Pamela's name into the conversation, she'd been enjoying the closeness of friendship; she'd felt as though she were helping him with a problem she herself had faced, and talking about it had helped her, too. Friendship between two colleagues: she honestly hadn't felt anything else right then. But had she messed up by dashing away so quickly? And had he wondered why she had dashed away?

That's when she'd phoned Abigail for a heart-to-heart chat — and advice. Her best friend had advised her to forget it.

'Honestly, Rose, if he thought anything at all, he probably thought you were worried about being late for work. You're letting that man get under your skin. What you need is a light flirtation. Thomas has taken on a locum vet. He's blond, rugged, brawny and single — and new to the area, like you, so . . .'

Rose had laughed and told her friend

that she wasn't in the market for a brawny vet.

'Stick to knitting bootees instead of trying play matchmaker, Abigail,' she chuckled. 'But thanks anyway.'

Now, though, as she prepared for the Mother and Baby Clinic, Rose wondered if Abigail was right. Maybe a light flirtation with a brawny vet would do her good. 'All work and no play,' she murmured as she checked the contents of the treatment trolley, making sure that whatever Matthew might need, it was be there.

She loved her work, though. At least, she loved being a nurse; it was too soon yet to know whether she enjoyed being a practice nurse here.

This afternoon's clinic would help her to decide that. Mother and Baby Clinics had always been one of her favourites. Hopefully she'd derive the same pleasure working with Matthew Knight as she had with the doctors where she'd worked before. As long as there weren't too many undercurrents

because of what had happened yesterday. And all the other yesterdays.

Or was she making mountains out of
molehills?

She'd soon know. In a few minutes
she'd be working alongside him. Then
she'd know if they were able to create
the right sort of atmosphere for their
patients — make the mums feel
confident and relaxed enough to ask
any questions and discuss any worries
they might have.

He'd arrived. She could hear him
chatting to the mums in the waiting
area.

Time to double-check the area she'd
prepared for herself: scales, height
charts, tape measure, a big unbreakable
mirror — babies were always intrigued
by seeing their own image, rattles,
squeaky toys, crayons, paper, her own
trolley . . .

She ran an experienced eye over the
trolley . . . yes, everything she'd need
was there.

She turned to her table. She put a

cassette player next to the pile of patient record cards. Should she play the tape? She'd no idea whether Matthew would approve of quiet, relaxing music in the background.

It's the mums and babies I should be thinking about, not him, she scolded herself. And in her experience, soft music helped.

She switched it on then searched in her bag for the tabard-style apron she always wore over her uniform during a baby clinic.

She'd just put it on when the door opened and Matthew came in.

'What's this?' He chuckled as he walked towards her. 'The latest fashion accessory for nurses?'

Laughter lines crinkled eyes bright with amusement and lifted the corners of his mouth attractively. He looked relaxed. At ease with himself. At ease with her?

'It serves a dual purpose,' Rose explained. 'It's waterproof so it protects my uniform and the babies are usually so fascinated by the brightly-coloured animals, it makes it easier for me to check them over.'

'They're brightly coloured all right.' Matthew put his hands on her shoulders, held her at arm's length and blinked furiously. 'I wouldn't like to work with you wearing that if I had a hangover. Where on earth did you get it?'

'I made it out of a plastic tablecloth.'

His hands were still on her shoulders. Her heartbeat didn't increase, her pulse stayed steady. No hidden undercurrents, either. Good — she'd be able to enjoy this clinic.

All of a sudden, her sense of fun bubbled over. 'Actually, I made a few more,' she told him. 'I've got a spare one with me. Interested?'

'Why not?' he replied easily. 'Can't have you stealing the show.'

She moved away from him and reached into her bag.

'Because that's what you've done,' he continued. 'You've made it all . . . ' He waved a hand, encompassing the toys, the bright height charts, the crayons and paper. ' . . . so that the mums and babies can enjoy coming here. You're even giving them music. It's good,' he added. 'Really good. Thank you, Rose.'

He smiled. It was a genuine smile of pleasure and respect and that was when her heart skipped a beat.

'I'm glad you like it.' She turned towards him, holding out the spare tabard. It was shocking pink. 'Take off your jacket and I'll slip this over your head.'

'It's even more garish than the one you're wearing.' He pulled a comical face as he draped his jacket over a chair. 'How come you happened to have a spare one with you anyway? Did you plan this?' he teased.

Her thumbs accidentally brushed his hair as she slipped the tabard over his head.

Liar, Rose Winter. It wasn't accidental at all.

'Do I take your silence as a yes, Rose?'

Had she planned on getting Matthew to wear the tabard? Not really.

'It was force of habit, bringing two with me,' she said. 'Simon, the doctor I did the baby clinic with where I worked before, always wore one. He wasn't as broad as you,' she added, praying that her face didn't look as flushed as it felt as she straightened the tabard across his chest. 'I'll have to make a bigger one for you,' she finished rather breathlessly.

She was trying to not to laugh at the sight of a bright green rocking horse, an orange kite and a pale pink bunny dancing across Matthew's ribs as he tugged the tabard down over his hips.

I wonder if she has any idea at all of how attractive she looks, standing there all pink-faced and giggly? Matthew wondered.

A lusty wailing from the waiting area put a stop to his thoughts.

'We'd best get started, Rose. There's more of a crowd than usual out there today. I think we're in for a hectic time. Who's first?'

Rose picked up the top record card. 'Mrs Dean, Alyssa-Marie and Abraham-James. And,' she chuckled, 'Nurse Chadwick has made a note: 'Mrs Dean likes the twins' full names to be used'.'

The Dean twins had been born prematurely and, at three months, were still tiny.

'But they're gaining weight,' said the proud mum, 'and they're ever so lively.'

'Abraham-James certainly is,' Matthew commented, amused. 'He's trying to pull the rocking horse off my apron.'

'They both reach out for the mobile above the cot,' said Mrs Dean, 'and they're fascinated by their hands.'

Rose was fascinated by Matthew's hands as she watched them moving over the small body. Her glance travelled from his fingertips to the dark hairs that shadowed his wrists and forearms. Her breath caught in her throat. She quickly turned her gaze to

131

the baby girl she was holding, stroking the soft downy head.

'That's the only problem.' Mrs Dean sighed. 'Alyssa-Marie's cradle cap. Abraham-James hasn't had it. Have either of you any tips on how I can get rid of it?' She looked from Rose to Matthew. 'I've tried washing her hair more often, washing it less often, oiling her scalp with baby oil, keeping a cotton hat on at night . . . nothing seems to shift it.'

'Coconut oil might help,' said Rose as, with a nod from Matthew, they exchanged babies. 'Rub it in gently, leave it overnight and then wash it out with a mild baby shampoo the following morning.'

'It's worth a try, Mrs Dean,' Matthew agreed. He smiled across at Rose and her heart pitter-pattered.

Rose smiled back, glad he hadn't glowered or commented adversely on her suggestion, then quickly lowered her eyes and got on with weighing and measuring Abraham-James.

'They're both coming on beautifully, Mrs Dean.' Matthew gave her back the baby girl and watched as she put her into the twin buggy next to her brother.

'Unless you have any problems, we'll see you again in a couple of weeks,' he added, opening the door and rolling his eyes at Rose as a crescendo of noise reached them.

★   ★   ★

There was a lot to get through. Matthew didn't waste any time but he didn't once show any sign of rushing, either. It was a quality Rose admired in him as he listened to problems, examined babies and took time to admire the squiggles that numerous toddlers made on the paper Rose had provided.

Several mums mentioned the music and the extra little touches Rose had brought to the clinic. Matthew responded with teasing quips at these times: 'Oh, we knew Nurse Rose would be brilliant, that's why we let her come and work here.' Or one that made Rose blush: 'She's not just a pretty face, is she?'

Things started to change when Penny Bryant bounded in with baby Adam in his buggy and a huge bunch of flowers nestling in the crook of her elbow.

'These are for you, Nurse Rose,' she said, handing her the bouquet, 'with love from Adam and me and his dad. I walked here today,' she added, smiling as Rose thanked her. 'You were so right about getting Adam out in the fresh air and about massaging him and the music and everything. That's one of the tapes you've got on now, isn't it? We've played them all. The 'go-to-sleep-baby' one is fantastic.'

Penny turned her attention to Matthew. 'It was like a miracle, Nurse Rose getting into my car and sorting me out. I felt really bad. There I was, bawling like a baby myself, and Nurse Rose sat with me for ages listening to my moans and groans. Then she came up with all these marvellous ideas to save my sanity.'

'When did this miracle take place?' Matthew asked and Rose was aware of a sudden tenseness about him.

'Tuesday morning in the car park,' Penny answered with a huge grin. 'Hard to believe things have changed so much in just a couple of days. I mean . . . ' she lifted Adam from the buggy, ' . . . he still has his little yelling sessions but not as often and they don't go on for as long. We even got five hours' sleep last night.' She laughed. 'We would have got a bit more but when I woke up and saw what time it was, I had to pick him up to check he was OK.'

'I'm so glad things are improving.' Rose smiled down at the baby. 'Now, you're due for your post-natal examination, Penny, so pop into the cubicle. Then Dr Knight can check you while I weigh and measure Adam.'

'I was telling some of the other mums about baby massage,' Penny said as she got undressed. 'They'd love to learn more about it. Are there any books or videos on it, Nurse Rose?'

'I'll get a list and let you have it next time you come,' Rose replied. 'Or you could go to the library, Penny. If they haven't got anything on the shelves, they'd order something for you.'

'Last time I went to the library, Adam yelled the place down. I felt so embarrassed I left without any books. But I'll call in tomorrow and show the librarians the new improved Adam.'

'Is he OK, Doctor?' Penny asked when Matthew walked into the cubicle with the baby in his arms.

'Everything is fine,' he replied. 'Nurse Winter can take him now and I'll have a look at you.'

So it's back to Nurse Winter. Rose sighed as she walked over to the scales. I wonder what's rattled his cage? Penny enthusing about baby massage?

'No, surely not,' she whispered, smiling, as Adam gripped her finger. 'Something has, though. We'd best get you weighed and measured so we're all ready when he's finished with your mum, hmm?'

Matthew only found one slight problem when he examined Penny; her muscles weren't firming up too well.

'That's because I haven't been doing my exercises,' she admitted. 'I was too tired and depressed. But now, thanks to Nurse Rose, I've got a happier baby and I'll have the time and energy to do them.'

An uncomfortable silence fell between Matthew and Rose after Penny left. Rose busied herself tidying the examination area. She was pleased that her suggestions had helped the young mother but she wished Penny hadn't been quite so profuse in her thanks.

'It makes me feel like Mrs Too-Good-To-Be-True,' Rose muttered, straightening the curtains with more force than was necessary.

'Whereas I feel just the opposite.' Matthew slid Penny's record card into its buff envelop then aimed it at the wire tray at the far end of his desk. He missed.

Rose bent to pick up the envelope. She wasn't sure what Matthew meant by his remark, but she knew their earlier camaraderie seemed to have disappeared.

'The opposite?' she queried.

'You said you felt like Mrs Too-Good-To-Be-True.'

'Oh, but I was talking to myself. I just . . . it was . . . '

He leaned back in his chair and watched her colour come and go as she fiddled with the envelope. Now he'd embarrassed her. He hadn't meant to do that. He was trying to put something right, for heaven's sake. Now he'd made matters worse.

How was it that they could never stay on an even keel with each other? How was it that these misunderstanding seemed to keep rising up between them? It was like taking two steps forward then one step back. All the time — yesterday in his car and now today.

138

'You make me feel like Mr Too-*Bad*-To-Be-True,' he snapped. 'You were late on Tuesday morning because you'd been talking to Penny Bryant. Right?'

'I couldn't just walk away and pretend I hadn't noticed her sobbing her heart out,' Rose protested, flinging the envelope into the wire tray.

'Drat it, Rose, I wasn't suggesting you should have done.' He banged clenched fists against his head. 'This is exactly what I mean. Why do you always think I'm getting at you?'

'I don't think that!'

'On Tuesday, when I pointed out that you were late, why didn't you tell me what had made you late? Did you really think I wouldn't understand?'

'No, of course I didn't. It was just — '

'And yesterday, when you dashed off in a huff . . . When I said you were soft and cosy, I was trying to explain how that would make Rosie feel good — I didn't mean it as a sexist remark.'

Rose regarded him. His statement

was so incongruous when he was sitting there wearing a bright pink apron patterned with rocking horses, kites, rabbits and teddy bears

Her lips twitched. She felt a bubble of laughter rising up. She fought to stop it from bursting out — fought and lost.

'I'm glad you think it's amusing — I'm trying to apologise!' Matthew said icily.

Still grinning, Rose picked up the big mirror and turned it to face him. 'Just take a look at yourself,' she told him. 'Then you'll understand why I could never think of you making a sexist remark. And,' she added, 'you don't need to apologise for anything. It takes two to cause misunderstandings and — '

'And two to make up,' Matthew finished for her.

Smiling, she put the mirror back. 'Now that's sorted, the two of us had better get on and see the last of the mob,' she said.

'OK,' he agreed, standing up and stretching.

Rose made a big deal of pulling the next patient record card out of its envelope. She had to do something to keep her eyes off those rippling shoulder muscles.

'Just one thing first, Rose. I'm sure you mentioned knowing someone who's experienced in baby massage.'

Rose nodded. 'Lucy. My godmother. Why?'

'Do you think you could arrange for her to come and give the mums a demonstration sometime?'

'She'd love that,' she told him.

'Good.' He smiled and took the record card from her hands. 'Come on, then — we'd better get on with it.'

Watching him walk to the door, Rose felt happy that they were friends again, but there was an underlying sadness, too; a sadness she refused to question in case she didn't like the answer.

★　★　★

The rest of the clinic flew by for Rose and before she knew it, she was closing the door behind the last patient.

'So that's it. Mother and Baby Clinic over for another week. It isn't always as busy as this one has been,' Matt said with a sigh.

'I enjoyed it,' Rose told him. 'Look at the mess of the place now, though.'

'It won't take long to tidy up with the two of us to do it.' Matthew bent and started picking up the toys. As she joined him, he said, 'There's something I want to ask you, Rose.'

'Fire away.'

'You know it's the school's Harvest Festival service tomorrow afternoon? You're only on duty until two o'clock. I checked. So I presume you'll be going?'

'I'd never hear the end of it from Pippa if I didn't go. Aren't you?'

Matt nodded seriously. 'Yes, but Pamela's got a tooth abscess — she's in agony and won't be able to come. Rosie will be singing her solo, but I'm worried she'll find it too much.' His eyes

142

clouded. 'I don't suppose you and I could go together so you can sit next to me and hold my hand? Metaphorically speaking, that is,' he added. 'We don't want to give Miss Peplow any reason to talk.'

'We'd better go in our own cars in case you get called away,' said Rose. 'But of course I'll sit with you.' She touched his arm. 'And try not to let Rosie know you're worried. You don't want her picking up any bad vibes from you.'

He nodded. 'I'm sure she'll be glad to know 'Pippa's Auntie Rose' has agreed to sit with me,' he said. 'She thinks you're the bee's knees. And I second it. You're a good friend, Rose.'

'Glad I can help,' she said. 'See you tomorrow.'

They said goodnight and as she made her way out of the building, Rose pondered on her renewed feeling of sadness. It's ridiculous to feel like this, she scolded herself. The clinic went well, Matt's great to work with, we cleared the air between us, and he said I'm a good friend. So what is there to feel sad about?

It wasn't anything to do with the fact that she and Matthew could never be more than just friends. Was it?

The Harvest Festival

'Hazelnuts, apple, rye bread, vine leaves, eggs, seeds in soil, turnip,' Pippa chanted as she watched Rose place everything into a round basket decorated with dried grasses. 'I hope I remember to say it in the right order when I have to tell the audience what my h-a-r-v-e-s-t gifts are,' said Pippa. 'I practised saying it for ages before I got up.'

'I've stuck a circle of paper with a number on it on to every gift.' Rose pointed to the bag of nuts. 'Start at number one — '

'Hey, that's a clever idea, Auntie Rose. Number one is 'h' for hazelnuts, number two is 'a' for apple . . . it's brilliant! Now I know I'll get it right.'

'I'm going to sit next to Rosie's uncle,' said Rose. 'You can look for us in the audience and I'll mouth the

145

words with you.'

'There's something else that will be a bit scary,' said Pippa. 'I'll have to stand behind the curtains on the stage 'till it's my turn. There'll be girls and boys from other classes there and I can't remember all their names.'

'I'm not surprised. You've only been at the school for a few days.'

'And we've only lived here for a week,' said Pippa. 'Well, it will be a week tomorrow 'cos we moved in on Saturday. It seems like ages, though.'

Rose nodded. It did feel like they'd lived here longer. She couldn't believe that today would be only her fourth day of working at the health centre, either.

'I think this house is glad we came to live in it,' Pippa continued. 'We've made it all cosy and homely already. I like the way the sun shines through the kitchen window on to the copper pans and I like how we've hung dried herbs on the hooks on the beams where people used to hang meat. I'm glad we

146

don't hang meat from them though!

'And I like the garden and the meadows with their daisies and clover and yellow rock rose flowers and the miles of moors where the sheep walk round patches of big ferns and purple heather . . . and . . . everything.'

'I'm sure the house and the garden and the meadows and hills are all glad we came to live here,' said Rose.

'Do you think my school likes me going there, Auntie Rose?'

'I'm sure it does, Tiddlywink.'

'So I must make sure I do everything right at the Harvest Festival.' Pippa fiddled with the dried grasses in the harvest basket.

Rose wondered if the coming event was the main thing worrying Pippa, or if the little girl was worried that everything would be snatched away from her again.

'Shall I put a helping stone in your pocket?' she suggested. 'A yellow topaz to help stop you feeling anxious?'

Pippa gazed up at her. 'Is there a

stone that helps you to know if it would be OK to tell a fib?' she asked quietly. 'Just a little fib,' she added.

Rose crouched down in front of her. 'Who do you want to tell this little fib to?' she asked.

'Rosie,' said Pippa. 'She wants to sing the harvest hymn 'cos it was her daddy's favourite hymn, but she's really, really worried it'll make her cry again.'

So Matthew was right, thought Rose.

'Rosie isn't a cry baby,' Pippa went on, 'she just gets so sad sometimes. Anyway, I thought if I fibbed and said I was extra sure she wouldn't cry, then she might not. But . . . ' Pippa pursed her lips and shook her head. ' . . . but really I think she might.'

Rose pulled Pippa to her and held her close. 'Maybe there's something else we could do for Rosie. How about me finding her a special helping stone, too? You know which one would be good . . . the pink one I've got. The rose quartz.'

'That's a brilliant idea.' Pippa's face lit up. 'I can show her my yellow stone and get her all interested and then tell her you sent one for her, too. And the rose quartz is like your name and like her name.'

Rose could never make up her mind if it was the idea of a helping stone that seemed to work for Pippa, or if it really was the 'power' of a particular crystal or gemstone.

The rose quartz was said to help heal emotional pain, so, as well as its name making it an ideal helping stone for Rosie, its special quality could be an additional benefit.

'OK.' Rose ruffled Pippa's hair. 'You move the harvest basket off the table and get the cereal out while I fetch the stones.'

On her way upstairs, Rose came to a decision. The hens she'd promised Pippa were coming from Thomas and Abigail's smallholding. She would phone Thomas and ask him to bring them tomorrow. The original plan had been to get the goats first. But they were a week away from getting Grizelda and Topsy.

Rose had felt very touched to hear of Pippa's concern for her new friend. She was a kind little girl and she was so looking forward to having the hens to look after. Why not let her start right away?

It was Abigail who answered the phone. Keeping her voice low in case Pippa came upstairs, Rose quickly explained things.

'Sounds like a good idea,' Abigail agreed. 'I expect Thomas will get Aidan to give us a hand.'

'Aidan?'

'The blond, rugged, brawny and unattached locum vet.' Abigail chuckled. 'He's staying with us until he can move into his flat. You'll like him, Rose, I just know you will.'

'I haven't got time right now to dissuade you from trying to play Cupid,' said Rose. 'I've got to get Pippa and her harvest basket to school.'

'OK, see you tomorrow. Wear something alluring!'

And before Rose could comment, her friend hung up.

Shaking her head, Rose opened the top drawer of her dressing table to find two tiny velvet bags, then picked out the yellow topaz and the rose quartz from amongst the crystals and gemstones she kept in a pretty box on top of the dressing table.

'You were a long time,' Pippa said when Rose returned to the kitchen. 'I've finished my cereal. I'll go and clean my teeth while you eat your cereal. Eat it quickly, Auntie Rose. We don't want to be late.'

*   *   *

Rose's morning passed in a whirl of taking blood pressures, removing stitches, syringing ears and changing dressings. Bert Jackson arrived for his third treatment and admitted grudgingly that his leg was starting to look a bit better.

Ellen, the lollipop lady, came to be weighed and was delighted to find she'd lost weight.

'Nearly six pounds,' Rose said as she filled in the weight record card. 'You're doing well, Ellen.'

'And you seem to be settling in nicely,' said Ellen. 'I was sitting next to old Bert Jackson in the waiting area and he was singing your praises. I didn't see your young 'un this morning; she isn't poorly, is she?'

'No, Pippa's fine. I drove her all the way today so I could carry her harvest basket into school for her.'

'That's all right then.' Ellen slipped her shoes and coat back on and sat opposite Rose. 'I met Penny Bryant pushing baby Adam out in his buggy yesterday afternoon — she lives a few doors down from me and George. She said how you'd helped her. Talking things over can help a lot sometimes.'

Rose looked up sharply. Was that a hint? She noted the way Ellen was twisting her wedding ring round and round.

'What is it, Ellen?' she asked gently. 'Is there something worrying you too?'

'It's my sister-in-law,' Ellen burst out. 'Her hubby — my eldest brother — died a year and a half ago. He was eighty, not that old by today's reckoning, but it was a natural death, he hadn't been ill, so it was a shock of course.

'She found it hard to cope with for the first couple of months. She cried so much she made her eyes sore and she had to get some drops from Dr Sinclair. Apart from that, she's hardly ever had a thing wrong with he. She's much younger than he was.' Ellen sighed and twisted her ring once more.

'And now?' Rose prompted.

'She's tired all the time, and she's gone ever so thin, though she says she's eating. And she says it isn't but I think clumps of her hair are coming out. It's hard to argue with her, she used to be a nurse. That's how she met Arthur — he was on her ward when he broke his leg. I keep on at her to come and see Dr Sinclair but she insists there's nothing wrong.'

'It certainly sounds as if she needs to see the doctor,' said Rose.

'Thing is,' Ellen continued, 'your Pippa mentioned that you'll be getting some hens in a few weeks. The kiddies tell me all sorts of things while they're waiting to cross the road.' She smiled briefly. 'Anyway, Sarah's got this really good hen-house; it's a fancy one, more like a Wendy house really. She was thinking of keeping hens herself before Arthur died. Now she wants a home for it and I wondered if you'd like it for when you get your hens. My George could deliver it for you. I thought if you went to look at it you could maybe . . . '

The words tailed away and Ellen looked hopefully at Rose.

'You want me to persuade her to come and see Dr Sinclair?' asked Rose.

'I want you to see if you can get her to talk. I reckon it's prolonged grief causing everything and she won't talk to me about Arthur, doesn't mention his name any more. It's not natural. But sometimes people open up to strangers, don't they — say things they wouldn't to family and friends?'

'I've already got hen-houses,' Rose began, 'but I expect Pippa would like a fancy one,' she added when she saw Ellen's disappointed expression.

'I know you aren't getting your hens for a while, but how soon could you go?' Ellen spoke eagerly. 'Sarah's in most of the time. That's another thing — she doesn't go out any more except to the shops.'

'I could call round later today after the school's Harvest Festival,' said Rose. 'I'd have to bring Pippa, though. She isn't going to her out-of-school club.'

'If you waited for me to finish my home-time stint, we could all go to Sarah's together,' said Ellen. 'I could show the little 'un the hen-house and you could chat to Sarah.'

'Right, we'll do that,' said Rose. 'Actually,' she confided, 'I've arranged for our hens to come tomorrow. Pippa doesn't know, though, so don't say anything.'

'My lips are sealed.' Ellen smiled and stood up. 'Thanks, Nurse, I'd best let you get on now. But I've a weight off my mind as well as off my body today,' she said, as she bustled to the door.

When she'd seen her last patient Rose phoned through to Linda on Reception and asked if Dr Sinclair was free.

'He is,' Linda confirmed. 'He's just taken a coffee through to his room.'

Rose walked along to Harry Sinclair's door and popped her head round. 'Can you spare a few minutes?' she asked.

'Of course. Anything to put off the paperwork! Come and sit down. Is this a social visit or have you got a problem?'

'It might be a problem, I'm not sure yet,' she said, and went on to tell him about her conversation with Ellen.

'You surely aren't worried that I might not like the idea of you talking to Sarah Carter?' Harry demanded.

'No, it's not that,' Rose protested. 'It's just — I'm sure I'll want to try to get Sarah to come for a check up. If she agrees it would be best if she could be seen quickly in case she changes her mind. You're duty doctor tomorrow and I know Saturdays are meant to be for emergencies only but . . . '

'If you can get Sarah to come, I'll see her. And it's good to know you care enough to offer to talk to her in your free time,' he added.

'It wasn't so much that I offered, it was more like I let myself be talked into it by Ellen.' Rose pulled a rueful face. 'I've got a feeling that if I have Sarah's hen-house — which I don't really need — I'll also be talked into getting more hens by my niece.'

'I believe she and Matt's niece have become best friends,' Harry said. 'Matt was telling me yesterday how he's decided to let young Rosie go to the out-of-school club with your Pippa. It's a grand idea, it'll give Pamela a break — I think she finds it hard to cope. And it'll do Rosie good to have a new interest, though I think getting the puppy helped her a lot.'

That reminded Rose that she wanted to tell Matt about the 'helping' stone she'd sent for Rosie. So after a few more words with the kindly senior partner, she excused herself and went off to see if Matt had finished surgery. She had time for a quick word before meeting up with Julia and Shirley to carry out the Friday stock check.

'He's gone on an emergency call,' Linda told her when she asked about Matt. 'Audrey's fitting in the rest of his patients.'

I just hope there'll be time to talk before we leave for the Harvest Festival, thought Rose. She wasn't too sure how Matthew would feel about the helping stone and she didn't really want to bring it up while they were sitting in the school hall.

*   *   *

It was quarter past two before Matthew returned. He hurried to the staff room and found Rose flicking through a magazine.

'Sorry I cut it so fine,' he said from the doorway. 'I had to drive Pamela to the dentist and on the way back a flock of sheep decided the road was a better place to be than the moor.'

'It seems to be a local hazard,' said Rose, putting down her magazine. 'It always amazes me they don't cause serious accidents.'

'They caused my blood pressure to rise, that's for sure,' said Matthew. 'You look nice,' he added. 'Very autumnal.'

'Thank you,' said Rose. The burnt orange top and the brown calf-length skirt patterned with swirls of green, orange and ochre had been Pippa's choice.

'After you,' he said when she reached the door. The scent of his aftershave invading her nostrils, her thanks came out as a husky whisper; she tried to keep as much distance between them as she slid past him.

'We'll go out the side entrance,' said Matthew. 'We'll be less likely to get waylaid by someone wanting a quick on-the-spot consultation.'

As they walked across the car park, Rose was painfully aware of the figure at her side. Weak rays of afternoon sunlight caught the silver threads in Matthew's dark hair. She liked the way his ears sat close to his head. There was just a faint darkness shadowing his jawline and the part of his throat visible above the dark green of his sweater. His well-cut jacket enhanced the broadness of his shoulders and the stone-coloured Chinos emphasised the length of his legs.

Her mouth felt dry and she flicked her tongue across her lips — just as Matthew turned his head to say something. For a brief moment their eyes locked and, as Matthew's darkened, Rose felt a gamut of emotions whirl through her.

She began to walk faster, but stumbled, and his arm shot out. The touch of his fingers — warm through the material of her top — made her skin tingle.

'Steady,' he said, 'we're not in that much of a hurry. I have to confess part of me is dreading getting there.' He stepped back and leaned against the Range Rover. 'I'm still worried it will be too much for Rosie. Her mum and dad both loved this time of year. They met at a Harvest Home . . . you know, a celebration party on a farm when the harvest has all been gathered in. Rosie loved hearing about that. This is her first autumn without Jonathan and Petra.'

'I sent her a helping stone,' said Rose, though she hadn't meant to blurt it out like that.

'A what?' asked Matthew.

'It's something I do for Pippa when she feels anxious about things. I give her a stone to put in her pocket and we call it a helping stone. Pippa needed one this morning and when she told me Rosie was worried in case she cried when she sang her solo . . . '

'Is this something you thought of, Rose, or is it one of your alternative therapies?'

Rose fiddled with the cuff of her sleeve. 'There is such a thing as crystal and gemstone therapy,' she said. 'I don't honestly know what I feel about it. Someone gave me a few stones when Pippa was in hospital. I took them to show her and one of the nurses saw them and told us each stone had its own special property. Pippa liked the idea of a stone helping her and . . . well . . . if having one in her pocket does help . . . ' She shrugged. 'I'm sorry if I stepped out of line.'

'I can remember when I was a kid finding a stone on the beach and putting it in my pocket.' Matthew smiled. 'Five minutes later the sand-castle I'd built won first prize. I was sure that stone had brought me luck. I kept it for years. I even . . . ' She saw his face colour slightly. 'I even took it to med school with me and put it in my pocket when I sat my exams. And if we don't get a move on,' he added, levering himself away from the car, 'we'll need a helping stone to get us there on time.'

★ ★ ★

Friday was market day in Morden. The traffic was quite heavy. Rose was glad she had to concentrate on her driving; it stopped her from thinking about Matthew.

She had a problem finding somewhere to park when they reached the school and all the time the precious minutes were ticking by.

When they finally entered the school hall, there was standing room only.

'Rose and Pippa will be able to pick us out easily enough, though,' said Rose. 'You're head and shoulders above everyone else.'

'That could be because it's mostly

females here.' Matthew sounded amused.

Rose hadn't really noticed that; she'd had to move up to make room for someone to stand at her other side and now she was only conscious of his closeness, of their bodies touching.

'It's hot in here, isn't it?' said the woman standing beside her.

Rose nodded. If her face looked as warm as it felt, she hoped Matthew would put it down to the heat of the hall, too.

The murmur of voices died away as Miss Peplow appeared on the stage to give her welcoming speech.

'And,' she concluded, 'to celebrate this year's Harvest Festival we have a short play.'

There were a few giggles and shuffles, then the curtains opened to reveal a haystack and two children dressed as farmers, each with a cardboard pitchfork. Then, one by one, the children walked on to the stage with a harvest gift. They all said a few words about their offering before going to sit by the haystack.

Pippa was word perfect and Rose felt a surge of pride. But when she put her harvest basket by the haystack, instead of sitting down, Pippa ran off-stage.

Rose frowned. Was there something wrong?

Pippa soon reappeared — leading Rosie by the hand.

'Now,' said Pippa, in a clear, confident voice, 'my best friend, Rosie, is going to sing a very special harvest song.'

Without thinking about it, Rose felt for Matthew's hand and held it tight.

Rosie stepped forward. Half-a-dozen children with recorders appeared from behind the haystack. They played a few notes, and then Rosie's voice soared out loud and clear: 'First the farmer sows his seed . . . '

Everyone in the hall — even Matthew after a husky start — joined in with the chorus . . . 'Oats, peas, beans, and barley grow . . . '

When the song ended, Rose wasn't

the only one to wipe away a tear. She let go of Matthew's hand but didn't look at him; she could feel the tension in his body and guessed he was thinking of his brother and sister-in-law.

The hall filled with applause and the children beamed down from the stage, waving to whoever had come to see them.

Eventually people began to make their way out of the hall. Miss Peplow had asked the adults to go to the classrooms to pick up their children.

'I'm just sorry Pamela wasn't here to see Rosie,' said Matthew as he and Rose joined the throng making their way to the classrooms. 'She'd have been so proud of her.'

Rose felt as though he'd thrown a bucket of cold water over her. She knew Matthew had only asked for her company and her support because his wife had been unable to come with him, but it still hurt to be reminded that she was so unimportant to him.

'I know you'll understand if I hurry

Rosie away as soon as I find her,' he continued, 'I'm sure she'll want to thank you for her helping stone, but I've got a clinic at four-thirty and I need to spend some time with her and Pamela first.'

Before Rose could answer, a crowd of excited children surged between them and they became separated. She didn't attempt to catch him up.

She'd accepted, of course, that he could never be more than a friend. But now she wasn't sure she even wanted friendship between them. It was too painful to keep playing second fiddle like this.

She already had friends, good friends — and maybe tomorrow she would make a new one, too, she thought suddenly. Abigail obviously liked Aidan; she wouldn't have had him staying at her house if she didn't. And if Abigail thinks I'll like him, too, mused Rose, I probably will.

Plans For Picnics

'Sunday barbecues seem to have become a habit,' said Rose. She and Abigail were preparing salads and dips in the kitchen while Thomas and Aidan slaved over the hot coals in the garden.

'How about Aidan, is he going to become a habit too?' asked Abigail. 'This is the second weekend you've seen him.'

'Last week was down to you, though — it was your idea to get him to help with the hens, remember. And I didn't suggest he brought Grizelda and Topsy yesterday, he did. I couldn't *not* invite him today when he's been so helpful.'

'You haven't answered my question, Rose.'

Rose took a pan of eggs off the cooker and walked to the sink to run cold water over them. Aidan was good-looking, had a great personality, and was fun to be with. He was twenty-eight, a year older than her, and Pippa liked him, but . . .

'I feel like I'm his auntie as well as Pippa's,' she told Abigail. 'I'm sure he'll make someone a fantastic boyfriend, though. Maybe I should introduce him to Linda at work. She saw me with him at the garden centre last week, when we were getting some extra chicken wire, and she hasn't stopped drooling since.'

'And you were accusing me of trying to play Cupid!' Abigail chuckled. 'First you fix my mother up with Harry Sinclair . . . '

'Hey,' Rose protested, as she shelled the eggs, 'that was nothing to do with me. They fixed themselves up all on their own.'

'But if you hadn't invited her to the health centre to meet the doctors and make arrangements for the baby massage session, they'd probably never have met.'

Rose smiled as she recalled that day. It had been obvious from the moment they shook hands that there was going to be something special between Harry Sinclair and Lucy. They were both here today, and had taken Pippa and the goats for a walk.

'Abi, you don't mind about your mum and Harry, do you?' Rose glanced at her friend.

'I think it's fantastic. Harry's been on his own since his wife died ten years ago and Mum's had fifteen years of being single. That's way too long. Everyone needs a special someone, Rose. I wish you could find someone, too. That's why I'd hoped you and Aidan . . . '

'At the moment I'm happy for it to be just me and Pippa,' said Rose. 'And the goats and the hens,' she added. 'This new way of life, including my job, is taking a bit of getting used to, without the complication of a new man, too.'

'You like working at the health centre, though, don't you?' Abigail looked up from slicing the eggs. 'You're getting on OK with Dr Knight now, aren't you?'

'Abigail, you're starting to sound like Pippa, asking more than one question at a time,' Rose protested. She did enjoy working at the health centre, and now that she had her diploma, she was looking forward to holding regular counselling clinics, too. Audrey Gordon was beginning to take an interest in complementary therapies and occasionally asked for suggestions for some of her patients. Rose was also starting to think of the two other practice nurses as friends . . .

But she didn't want to answer the question about Matthew. She wasn't sure how they were getting on, not really. When she assisted him at the clinics, they worked together easily enough. If she needed him to check one of her patients, he never queried her sending for him. If he needed her to fit in one of his patients, he always made a point of thanking her for shuffling her list.

He treated her politely whenever they met up in the staff-room and was always willing to talk over any problems regarding patients.

Things had changed since the Harvest Festival, though. It was partly her own fault, because she'd felt as if he'd used her, and partly because he didn't talk to her about Rosie any more. She knew he'd taken her to her parents' 'memory place', but he hadn't told her, Pippa had.

They bumped into each other a few times outside of work when they were picking up the girls from out-of-school club. They spoke, of course, but it was just polite words about the weather and mundane things like that. On these occasions, the cool way he treated her was emphasised by the way he talked and joked with Pippa.

Rosie always greeted 'Pippa's Auntie Rose' with huge enthusiasm and often asked for a big hug, too. Maybe that was it: maybe Matthew didn't like his niece wanting hugs from her.

Rose's heart was heavy. After the Harvest Festival, she'd thought that she didn't want friendship between them. Now she was mourning for the friendship that might have been.

'Wakey wakey, Rose! Here's Mum, Harry and Pippa back.' Abigail laughed as Harry knocked on the kitchen window and made eating actions with his hands and mouth.

Pippa dashed into the kitchen to tell Rose about the walk. 'Do you know the path outside our farmhouse is part of the Morden Centenary Way? We walked along it right to the end of the second big field and there's a gate you can go through and a baby waterfall to cross and then you're in the woods.'

'We didn't go in the woods,' said Lucy as she and Harry followed her into the kitchen. 'We thought we'd let Pippa take you there, Rose.'

'We'll go when it's my half-term,' said Pippa. 'It starts on Friday. You're swapping some hours with Nurse Shirley so you can have all day Friday off, aren't you, Auntie Rose? We could go in the woods then and take a picnic. Harry says it's going to rain at the end of the week but we can wear our wellies and waterproofs. Can we ask Rosie to come, too?'

'We'll see,' Rose replied. It would give her a chance to talk to Matthew about something other than work, she mused.

'I'm hungry,' said Pippa, 'but Thomas and Aidan said it'll be another ten minutes before the barbecue food is ready. Can I have one of our own eggs to eat while I'm waiting?'

'You asked just in time, Pips.' Abigail laughed. 'I was about to slice up the last one.'

'Hands, Pippa,' ordered Rose, pointing to the sink.

'Our hens laid sixteen eggs yesterday, in the hen-house Mrs Carter gave us,' Pippa reported as she washed her hands.

Rose glanced at Harry Sinclair. 'We took half a dozen eggs to Sarah Carter.

She's looking much better. She's a new person now she knows she isn't going blind. She can't wait to have her cataracts removed. The first one's being done next week.'

When she'd gone to Sarah Carter's to look at the hen-house, Rose had noticed immediately the slight greyness of Sarah's pupils. She'd waited for an opportune moment and then asked gently if Sarah had seen anyone about her cataracts.

The answer had been hysterical laughter, followed by tears. Sarah, who had once been a nurse, hadn't realised she'd got cataracts. She'd thought the shock of her husband's death was making her go blind. As a result, instead of remembering him with love, she'd started hating him for what his death had done to her.

She hadn't dared to talk about him in case the hatred showed.

She'd started to hate herself too, for feeling that way, and had been going round in a maze of misery; not eating properly, not going out, not caring about her appearance.

Now, though, all that had changed. Harry had made her a quick appointment with an eye specialist, and advised a tonic to build herself up, while Rose had asked Abigail, an expert on hair problems, to make up something to help Sarah's hair and scalp condition.

'What happened with Sarah is community networking at its best,' said Harry. 'Though the very best,' he added, smiling fondly at Lucy, 'was when Rose suggested you giving our mums a talk and demonstration on baby massage.'

'Aah, love's autumn dream,' Abigail whispered to Rose. 'Talking of which, let's go and see if the love of my life has got anything for us to eat yet.'

With Harry and Lucy so obviously a couple and Thomas keeping a loving and attentive eye on Abigail, Rose and Aidan sat together on the stone wall and chatted as they ate. Aidan made sure to include Pippa in the conversation, answering her many questions with good-natured thoughtfulness and the occasional joke that made the little girl giggle.

He really is one of the good ones, pondered Rose. I don't know why he doesn't light my fire. But he doesn't. Not the tiniest sparkle. But he'll make someone a wonderful husband and I bet he'll be a marvellous dad, too.

Later when Pippa was in bed and Aidan was helping Rose tidy up, he told her how much he appreciated her friendship.

'Me, too,' said Rose, smiling inwardly at his gentle way of telling her he didn't fancy her. 'And,' she added, 'if there's ever anyone special you want to bring here, she'll be more than welcome.'

Before her visitors left, Rose managed to get Abigail on her own and, chuckling, reported the conversation.

'Oh, well,' said Abigail, 'I suppose it is good sometimes to have a male just as a friend.'

Which brings me back to Matthew, Rose thought wryly. Perhaps I should stop waiting for him to talk about anything other than work and ask him how the puppy is settling in or something . . .

* * *

Rose didn't see much of Matthew over the next few days. She had decided to ask him during Thursday's Mother and Baby Clinic about Rosie coming on the picnic with Pippa. Perhaps he'd seem more approachable when he was wearing one of her colourful tabards.

To her surprise, though, it wasn't Matthew who arrived for the clinic. It was Audrey Gordon, who smiled as she explained the swap. 'Matt has talked so much about your extra little touches, Rose, I wanted to see them for myself.'

The clinic went well and all the mums seemed to be looking forward to the baby massage session the following week.

'You must be really pleased about it, Rose,' Audrey said as they tidied up the toys and books. 'I think we were a bit less enthusiastic than we could have been when you talked about baby massage at your interview. I wasn't at all receptive, I remember. I felt bad about it later; at the time all I could think about was my terrible PMT.'

'I'm sure Lucy would be able to recommend some useful massage and bath oils for that,' Rose said.

'I intend to do just that,' Audrey smiled. 'And I'm thinking about seeing a reflexologist.'

'Worth a try,' said Rose, glad that her first impression of Audrey's unfriendliness had been wrong.

'Right,' she added, looking round the now tidy room, 'all done and dusted for another week. Do you know if Matthew's around, Audrey?'

'He said he was going to catch up on paperwork and make a few phone calls,'

Audrey replied. 'I don't know if he's with his secretary or in his consulting room.'

'I'll try to catch him before I leave,' said Rose.

She didn't manage to see Matthew, though, and when she picked up Pippa from out-of-school club, Matthew had already fetched Rosie.

Pippa was disappointed. 'I thought you saw her uncle every day at work.'

'I do,' Rose replied, 'but I just haven't had a chance to talk to him.'

Pippa gave a huge sigh. 'I really, really wanted Rosie to come the first time we explored the woods.'

'Never mind, Tiddlywink. How about we have a picnic breakfast and a picnic lunch in the paddock tomorrow and save going to the woods for another day?'

'Picnics in the paddock would be fun, but when could we have one in the woods with Rosie?'

Rose smiled at her niece's one-track mind. 'You're on half-term all next week. I don't start until twelve on Wednesdays, remember. Maybe Rosie could come for a morning picnic in the woods then, and I could take you both to out-of-school club afterwards?'

'What if you don't get a chance to talk to Rosie's uncle again?'

'I'll make sure I get a chance on Monday. I'll leave a note on his desk to say he must not go anywhere until I've talked to him.'

'Brilliant,' Pippa said happily. 'It means I'll get three picnics instead of one.'

* * *

Rose woke early on Friday morning and turned over to face the window. The curtains were swaying gently which told her there was a breeze, but it wasn't light enough to see what else the weather was doing. Last night's local forecast hadn't looked good.

She slid out of bed and stuck her head out the window. It must have

181

rained in the night — she could smell damp grass and earth, Michaelmas daisies and bracken. But it wasn't raining now.

She had promised Pippa she'd make bread rolls for the breakfast picnic. If she started now, she would have time to make shortbread and a fruit slab as well, while the dough was rising.

By eight o'clock the smell of newly-baked fruit cake and bread filled the kitchen. Rose had milked Grizelda, and Pippa had gone to collect the eggs from the hens.

As Rose packed fruit, butter, jam, hard-boiled eggs, cheese, milk and fruit juice into a hamper — Pippa had insisted on the hamper, even though the paddock was right next to the farmhouse — she thought how good things were. But even so, she felt as though something were missing from her life. She tried to ignore the little voice in her head reminding her of Abigail's words: 'Everyone needs a special someone'.

It isn't that at all, Rose argued back

at the voice. It's the not knowing if we'll definitely be able to stay here.

If only she could hear that Richard's business was sold. The agent had said he had a prospective buyer for it; it was about time he put in an offer. Still, there was another five months to go before she would have to find the deposit for the farmhouse. It would be all right.

'It's got to be,' she muttered as she closed the lid of the hamper.

'What's got to be what?' asked Pippa, arriving back in the kitchen with a bowl full of eggs.

Rose grinned. 'What I've put in the hamper has got to be enough for our breakfasts,' she said.

It was a morning full of fun and laughter. Grizelda kept trying to eat the tablecloth Pippa had spread out on the grass in the middle of the paddock, Topsy knocked the milk over then bounded off with the cardboard carton in her mouth, and one of the hens flew on to the barn roof.

'It's Trudi,' said Pippa. The little girl had a name for every hen and knew exactly which one was which. 'How are we going to get her down? She's the boss hen and if we don't get her down, the others might fly up there with her.'

'I don't think she'll come down while we're here,' said Rose as she packed away the remains of the picnic. 'Put Grizelda and Topsy on their ropes and we'll take them for a walk. I'll sprinkle some corn around the paddock — that should tempt Trudi down,' she added.

'OK,' said Pippa. 'We could walk to the woods. I'll just show you where they are, we won't go in them.'

Rose glanced up at the sky. 'It's clouding over,' she said. 'We'd best put our wellies on and take our waterproofs in case it rains.'

★ ★ ★

Two hours later, when they'd shut the goats in their shed, Rose and Pippa stood on the footpath and stared up at

184

the barn roof. Trudi had somehow made her way over the top and down the other side. Clucking crazily and flapping her wings every now and then, she stared back at them.

'Do you think her feet are stuck in the gutter?' asked Pippa. 'That might be why she isn't flying down.'

'I think she's just being stubborn,' said Rose.

'What if she isn't? What if her claws are stuck? What if she's hurting and we're standing here not doing anything?'

Rose sighed. 'OK, I'll go and get a ladder. Trudi's close to the end of the guttering. I'll check her claws aren't stuck, then try to push her off sideways.'

'With any luck,' Rose muttered as she fetched the ladder, 'that dratted hen will fly down while I'm getting the ladder set.'

But Trudi stayed where she was.

'You're almost close enough to stretch your arm out and reach her feet,

Auntie Rose,' Pippa called encouragingly.

'One more rung . . . ' Just as Rose put one hand on the guttering, ready to slide along sideways, Trudi let out a loud squawk and, half-flying and half-jumping, landed on Rose's head, her claws digging in.

Startled, Rose jerked her head and screwed her eyes tightly shut as the ladder swayed ominously. Climbing up ladders had never been one of her favourite things.

Just as she was wondering if she could pluck up the nerve to climb down, Pippa let out a squawk to rival Trudi's.

'Look who's coming along the path, Auntie Rose! It's Rosie and her uncle and they've got the puppy with them.'

Rose's heart sank and she gently banged her head against a rung of the ladder. 'What have I done to deserve this? It's like a scene out of a farce. I've got to get down.'

She drew in a ragged breath then

slowly, arms and legs trembling, began her descent.

The children's shrill voices, the puppy's yapping, the hen's squawking and Matthew's deep baritone seemed to be coming from far away so she was surprised to feel firm, comforting hands on her waist.

She felt the ground beneath her feet and her first ridiculous thought was, Why did I have to be wearing unflattering yellow and green wellies?

'Are you OK, Rose?' Matthew swivelled her round to face him.

She nodded, unable to think of anything to say.

'Your head's bleeding.' She felt the gentle touch of his fingers in her hair.

'That darned hen. She flew on to the roof and I — '

'Pippa told me why you were up the ladder. You should have left the hen to come down on her own. And your head *is* bleeding, Rose. It needs cleaning. You could do with a strong, sweet cup of tea, too — you're trembling.'

His hands were on her shoulders now and Rose knew her trembling wasn't entirely down to her fright. He looked so strong, so masculine; she didn't want to move. She wanted . . .

'Auntie Rose, can Rosie and Sasha come into the paddock with me? Trudi's wriggling — I think she wants to go back to the other hens.'

Pippa's voice jerked Rose to her senses. She stepped away from Matthew to see Pippa holding Trudi and Rosie holding the puppy.

'Sasha's on her lead,' said Rosie. 'But Uncle Matt told me to hold her while he helped you down the ladder. I'll keep her on her lead if we can go into the paddock 'cos she might want to play with the hens.'

'Is that OK with you?' Rose asked Matthew.

'Only if you let me take you indoors to bathe your head and make you that cup of tea,' he said. 'I could do with a cuppa myself. When I planned the walk, I didn't realise how far it was.'

'So can we go into the paddock?' Pippa demanded impatiently. 'And can I let Grizelda and Topsy out? They're used to dogs from when they were at the Animal Rescue Centre.'

Rose nodded. 'As long as you both promise to be sensible,' she cautioned as the two little girls beamed their thanks.

'What a fantastic spot you live in,' said Matthew as he and Rose made their way to the house. 'I had no idea when I planned the walk that it would take us past where you live.'

'So where do you live?' Rose asked.

'Down in the valley, just off the main road, about a half-mile the other side of the woods,' he replied. 'But I'd love to get us something like this,' he added, as he followed Rose inside.

Rose led him into the kitchen and washed her hands before filling the kettle and plugging it in.

'First aid box, Rose?' he said determinedly. 'You need antiseptic on the scratches on your head.'

Rose knew he was right. She fetched the first aid box.

'I'll do it, you sit down,' he commanded.

Rose held herself rigid as his hand moved towards her head.

'Don't tell me you're scared it's going to sting,' he teased.

Better he thought that than him guessing at the forbidden feelings she was fighting to overcome. She could hear his watch ticking and concentrated on counting the ticks. Only seventy-eight, she realised in surprise when he said, 'There, all done. Now I'll make us that cup of tea.'

Rose closed her eyes . . . Heavens, she had to stop acting like a lovelorn teenager.

She opened her eyes and jumped to her feet. 'I baked this morning. Would you like a slice of fruit cake with your tea?'

'Would I!' He grinned. 'Walking always makes me hungry.'

Rose prepared a tray. 'We'll take it

through to the lounge,' she said. 'We can keep an eye on the girls then. I'll see if they want anything when we've had ours.'

Like the kitchen, the lounge was a welcoming, relaxing room. As he pulled out a small table for Rose to put the tray on, Matthew looked round with interest at the homely touches. Rose and Pippa's books lined dark oak shelves, bright, sweet-smelling scatter cushions adorned the chairs, and there were a few ornaments and photos along the mantelshelf. A brass hod and a copper cauldron, standing on opposite sides of the wide stone hearth, contained logs and coal, a tall brass jug held brightly-coloured spills and a fire was laid in the grate.

'Do you light the fire or is it just for show?' he asked.

'I light it most days, I love a real fire,' Rose replied. 'In fact, I'll light it now. It soon goes cool in here at this time of year.'

The sound of happy, high-pitched

voices and the occasional giggle reached them from outside.

Matthew picked up his cup of tea and a slice of cake and wandered over to the window. 'Mmm, this is good,' he said. 'Rosie's in her element out there.' He turned and propped himself against the windowsill. 'I really must look for somewhere like this for us to live.'

'Pippa and I love living here,' Rose confided. 'It was my sister and brother-in-law's dream house. I want to keep the dream alive for Pippa, but if Richard's business isn't sold soon, the house will be on the market.' She went on to tell him about the lease she'd negotiated.

'When . . . how did your sister and her husband die?' Matthew asked softly.

'In June. A motorway pile-up. Hannah, Richard and Pippa were on the way back from a day out and a coach ploughed through the barrier into their car. Hannah and Richard were killed outright. Pippa suffered a leg injury. It wasn't really the coach driver's fault,' Rose said, turning her gaze to the fire as it started to flicker into life. 'He had a heart attack, but I can't help blaming him sometimes.'

'I know what you mean.' Matthew's voice was rough with emotion. 'Rosie's parents — my twin brother and his wife — were on that coach. Yes,' he added when Rose looked at him in amazement, 'it is a grim coincidence, isn't it? I'd only been back in the area a couple of months. I'd been working in London for three years, but I never felt at home there and when Jonathan — my brother — told me the health centre was looking for an extra partner . . . '

Matthew sighed. 'At least we spent a lot of time together during those two months. I suppose that might comfort me one day.'

'Precious memories,' Rose murmured. She went to stand by him at the window.

'It's a small world, isn't it?' he said. 'Rosie and Pippa would never have met but for that crash. Rosie blames herself for her parents' death,' he continued. 'She reckons if she'd been with them, they would have been sitting in a different seat and wouldn't have been killed. It's hard to know what to say.'

'Pippa once said that the crash happened because she laughed and distracted Hannah,' said Rose. 'All either of us can do for them is to give them love and security. Children are resilient. I don't suppose Rosie or Pippa will ever forget what happened but they'll both be OK in time, I'm sure they will.'

Her hands tightened around her cup as they watched Rosie and Pippa trying to make Sasha and Topsy walk to heel.

'I've just got to keep this house for Pippa,' she said. 'But I don't know how I'll manage. I've got some savings, but not enough for the deposit needed on this sort of property . . .'

Silence fell and Rose felt her brow furrowing as her worries returned.

She shook her head and forced a bright smile. 'That's enough miserable talk for now! My tea's gone cold — I'll go and make a fresh pot.'

Matthew missed her presence, the feel of her shoulder against his arm, the second she walked away. Her light floral perfume lingered, mingling with the woody scent from the logs burning on the fire. He was building up too many memories of times they'd spent together. He ought to be going . . .

The rain pelting against the window startled him with its suddenness.

'Matt, I'll have to go and put the goats in,' Rose called from the kitchen. 'Could you go upstairs and grab some towels from the cupboard on the landing? The girls and Sasha will be soaking.'

★   ★   ★

Half-an-hour later, Sasha lay spread out in the hearthrug fast asleep as Matthew leaned over her and held a slice of bread on a toasting fork to the flames of the fire.

'This'll take ages,' he complained. 'The fire isn't hot enough yet.'

'But fire toast tastes much nicer than ordinary toast,' said Pippa. 'And it wouldn't be a proper lounge picnic if we made the toast in the toaster. I think this is better than the picnic in the woods I wanted Rosie to come to 'cos this one just happened when we didn't know it was going to happen.'

'And our walk turned out better than we thought it would because we found your house,' said Rosie.

'And look what I've found.' Rose came into the lounge carrying another toasting fork.

'Brilliant!' said Pippa. 'Now you and Rosie's Uncle Matt . . . ' She broke off and shook Matthew's arm. 'I can't keep saying 'Rosie's Uncle Matt' every time — it's too big.'

'Matt or Matthew is OK by me if it's OK by your auntie.' Matthew quirked an eyebrow at Rose.

Rose nodded. 'And Rosie can call me Rose instead of 'Pippa's auntie'.'

'Good! Well,' Pippa continued, 'you and Matthew can have races, Auntie Rose, to see who can toast the most slices of bread the quickest.'

'Matt has an unfair advantage,' Rose protested. 'He's closer to the fire.'

'He won't be if you move round and squash up close to him,' said Rosie.

Rose tried telling herself that it was all part of the fun, the sort of thing she'd do with Aidan. But it wasn't Aidan she was squashed against, was it?

Her breath caught in her throat whenever Matthew's shoulder brushed hers, or her hand brushed his. Their thighs kept rubbing, too, whenever one of them moved forward to reposition the bread on their toasting fork.

At last all the bread was toasted; the little girls counted the slices they'd buttered and declared the race a draw. Rose was relieved about that. At least she'd been spared paying or receiving a forfeit kiss. She felt a blush rise up her face at the thought of kissing Matthew.

'You and Matthew can have these slices, Auntie Rose,' said Pippa as she put her plate of toast on the small table in front of the settee. 'I'll sit on the rug with Rosie and we'll eat the toast she buttered.'

Rose scrambled to her feet and went to sit on the settee. Matthew wriggled round and spread his length on the floor, propping himself up on one elbow. Then he reached for a slice of toast.

'You look as warm as this toast, Rose,' he teased, looking up at her. Rose hoped he didn't guess why.

They all munched companionably. Sasha, still sprawled out on the hearthrug, dreamed and twitched in her sleep, the fire crackled and flickered and the rain was still pelting against the window. Rose had switched the lamps on earlier and their friendly glow added to the ambience. Now she was a comparatively safe distance away from Matthew, she wished this moment could last for ever.

But all too soon the plates were empty.

'You and me will take them into the kitchen, Rosie,' said Pippa, 'and then we'll find some board games.'

They played Ludo and Snakes and Ladders and Tiddlywinks. Then Sasha woke and stretched, and Matthew moved like lightning to pick her up. 'Got to get her outside before she makes a puddle,' he said, as he hurried out of the room.

Rose leaned back on the settee and watched Pippa and Rosie whispering and giggling together.

'We've decided . . . ' Pippa announced when Matthew returned with Sasha. 'We've decided we'll play Sardines. You can be first fish and go and hide, Auntie Rose. We'll count to two hundred and Matthew can come looking for you. Then . . . '

'Then we'll count to another two hundred and me, Pippa and Sasha will come and find both of you,' Rosie said excitedly. 'And we'll all end up squashed like sardines in a tin.'

Rose chose Pippa's favourite hiding place — the recess under the wide stone slab shelves in a large walk-in cupboard in the room behind the lounge. Whether Matthew found her or not, she knew Pippa would look here first.

She heard the girls finish counting the first two hundred aloud, then starting from number one again. She heard Matthew stomping around saying, 'Not here . . . not here.'

Then the cupboard door opened. He peered in and Rose saw him smile. He pulled the door almost shut again, then crawled into the recess to join her.

'I haven't had this much fun for years,' he whispered. He smelled of warm buttered toast and the aftershave that was so essentially him.

'I don't think I'll ever forget this afternoon,' he added.

'It has been good,' Rose whispered back. 'Hannah always wanted Pippa to do the same things she and I did when we were little. We never watched television much — we made our own fun.'

'Yes, Jon and I tended to do that, too,' said Matthew. 'Of course, being boys there was a fair amount of rivalry between us. But I like to think we were both good losers. Oh, Rose, I miss him so much.'

Without thinking, Rose laid her palm against his cheek. 'I know,' she murmured. 'I still find myself about to lift the phone to talk to Hannah, then reality hits me. We'll never stop missing them, Matt, but . . . as time goes on, the pain and emptiness might not be as sharp.'

She never knew whether she drew his face closer or if it was him who moved, but suddenly she felt the warmth of his mouth on hers. Little ghost kisses whispered against her lips; she lowered her hands to wind her arms around his neck, felt his hair brushing her fingers. She responded to his kiss like thirsty earth soaking up the rain . . .

The dream ended abruptly as Sasha, yapping excitedly, hurled herself against them. Rose dropped her hands and drew away from Matthew to Hear Pippa and Rosie giggling as they stood in the open doorway.

'Er . . . ' Rose stepped out of the recess, holding on to the stone cupboard walls for support. 'Matt had something in his eye . . . I was trying to get it out, but we couldn't see very well.'

'Then you kissed him better 'cos it was hurting, like you kiss me better if I've hurt myself,' said Pippa, as she and Rosie moved away.

'You're so lucky to have your Auntie Rose, Pippa,' said Rosie.

'You've got your Aunt Pamela,' Pippa pointed out.

'If I've hurt myself Aunt Pamela doesn't kiss me better, she just says, 'Brace up, Rosemary'. I think it's because she's old. She's my great-aunt, really, you know. She's Uncle Matt's aunt. She only came to help Uncle

202

Matt look after me when Mummy and Daddy died. She's going back to her own home soon.'

Rose felt a surge of delight rise inside her. She turned to look at Matthew as he came out of the cupboard. He wasn't married — she had no reason to feel guilty about that kiss, no reason to feel guilty for loving him. Yes, she could admit it now. She loved Matthew with all her heart and soul.

But he met her glance with cold eyes. 'It's time we were going,' he said. 'Could I trouble you to give us a lift home, Rose? I don't fancy walking through the woods in the dark and the rain.'

'Of course.'

Rose walked jerkily into the lounge, wondering why he was acting like this. Why was he so obviously regretting their closeness, their togetherness, their loving kiss?

He must think I'm looking for a meal ticket, she anguished. He thinks I threw myself at him, thinks I'm planning on marriage so I won't lose the farmhouse.

Well, if that's what he thinks of me, she raged, he isn't worth loving.

★ ★ ★

Matthew relived the afternoon at Rose's farmhouse many times over the weekend. He'd fallen for her in a big way. Looking back, it had probably happened the first moment they'd met when she'd been ferociously protecting his niece.

He'd fought the attraction, fought his feelings; he'd loved and lost before. After finding his fiancé with his best friend, he didn't do love any more. For a full year afterwards he'd never allowed — never wanted — a meaningful relationship.

Those feelings had still held good when he'd come home to Lancashire. No way was he going to let anyone into his life to hurt him again. Then, of course, he'd suddenly become responsible for Rosie and, for a while, there had been no time, no inclination for a relationship of any kind.

'Until I met Rose.' Those four words were driving him mad, echoing round his head — his heart — without relief.

Rose had crept deeper and deeper into his heart every day. It wasn't just because their circumstances were similar; it wasn't because of her natural empathy with Rosie. It was because she was Rose. Adorable, generous, kind, caring, warm, beautiful Rose. He ached for her.

He couldn't have started a relationship with her that wasn't meaningful. It would have to be all or nothing. And, until Friday afternoon, he'd forced himself to make it nothing.

It had been hard; he'd almost told her how he felt about her when they'd been talking about helping stones before they'd gone to the Harvest Festival. There hadn't really been time, though, and he'd been het up about Rosie as well. And after the Harvest Festival, he'd had to hurry off. Then, the following day he'd run into his ex-fiancée at a friend's wedding and all his distrust of women had flooded back.

He'd been pretty cool with Rose in the following days. But why? How could he have let the past affect his feelings for Rose?

'Stupid, stupid, stupid,' he berated himself.

But on Friday he'd realised just how much he and Rose had to offer each other. He wasn't blind, he could read the signs, he knew Rose had feelings for him. He guessed she'd been fighting them. Maybe she'd been hurt in the past, too, and didn't want to go there again.

Whatever, Friday afternoon had changed things. He'd thought — especially after that kiss, full of warmth and tenderness — that they were both ready to love and trust, ready to start something new and glorious.

Then Rosie had mentioned that Pamela was going back to her own home soon. He'd caught the look of quickly-hidden surprise, and something else he couldn't read, in Rose's eyes.

In that moment, he'd realised that whatever he did or said after that, Rose would think he only wanted her so she could help him with Rosie.

So there had been no point in telling Rose how he felt, no point in telling her he loved her like he'd never thought it possible to love anyone.

It was over.

He'd loved and lost again.

★   ★   ★

And now it was Monday morning. If he didn't see Rose dropping Pippa off at out-of-school club, he was bound to see her later at the health centre. He would smell her perfume when she walked by, hear her voice, and quite likely have to work with her.

Not only that. Now that Pippa and Rosie realised they lived quite near each other, they were sure to want to see each other at weekends and during holidays. That would mean he and Rose would be meeting, too — doing things together because of their nieces.

'Shoot,' he muttered.

In the back seat of the car, Rosie giggled. 'Are you remembering that game of Tiddlywinks on Friday, Uncle Matt, when Pippa yelled 'Shoot' every time she tried to flick a counter into the cup? You know, Friday was one of my bestest ever days. I love Pippa — and I love Rose, too, don't you?'

Out of the mouths of babes, thought Matthew as he grunted a non-committal reply.

Hidden Heartache

On Sunday, Rose woke with a splitting headache that soon turned into a roaring migraine. She and Pippa had arranged to spend the day at Lucy's house but, knowing she was in no fit state to drive, Rose phoned her godmother to explain why they wouldn't be going.

Lucy drove over straight away to give Rose a gentle massage before making her go and lie on the bed with the curtains closed.

'Don't worry about the animals,' Lucy ordered. 'Someone will come over this evening to milk Grizelda, feed the hens, and to check on you. Pippa can come with me now and stay overnight. Abigail says she'll take her to out-of-school club in the morning. And, remember, she'd already arranged to take her to the cinema this afternoon.'

'I'll fetch her around eight o'clock tomorrow evening,' Rose murmured, as she lay with eyes closed.

'We'll see how you are, Rose. If you're no better, there's no question of you going to work in the morning or fetching Pippa.'

'Your massage has helped already,' said Rose. 'Thanks. I'll probably sleep until tomorrow morning.'

* * *

I was right, thought Rose, when she woke up and glanced at the time. It's seven o'clock; I've slept for hours and hours. She sat up cautiously and moved her head from side to side. No pain, only a slight ache lingered at one side of her temple.

A shower, a cup of peppermint tea and a slice of toast would soon shift that, she decided, getting out of bed.

When she'd eaten her light breakfast, she put on her waterproof jacket and went across to the paddock to feed the hens and milk Grizelda.

The early morning air cleared away the last of the sore feeling from her sinus points and the hens and goats greeted her as if they hadn't seen her for weeks.

Back inside, she ran cold water over the milk container to cool it and then phoned Lucy to say 'Good morning' to Pippa and to assure Lucy her migraine had gone.

'So I'll be able to pick Pippa up from Abigail's this evening. Thanks for your help, Lucy.'

As she got ready for work a few minutes later, Rose wished that her heartache could be cured as well as her migraine.

If only she'd known from the start that Pamela was Matthew's aunt and not his wife, she would have acted differently on so many occasions.

That time in his car outside the school — she'd felt so close to him then, but she'd hurried away in case anyone had seen them and got the wrong idea.

At the end of the Harvest Festival she'd thought he was hurrying home to be with his wife. She'd felt used and hurt and there had been no reason to feel that way! She could have gone after him, or at least not been so cool towards him in the following days.

Rose circled her lips with one finger. The memory of Matt's kiss still lingered, the smell of him, the taste of him was still with her . . . and so was the cold look he'd given her when as he emerged from their hiding place.

It was all well and good saying that he wasn't worth loving if he thought she was trying to trap him into a relationship, to use him as a meal ticket. OK, she could say it and keep on saying it. That's what had caused her migraine — the continual telling herself that Matthew wasn't worth loving. The trouble was, she couldn't make herself mean it.

Still, she'd managed to stay cool and

merely professional towards him in the days following the Harvest Festival. She'd just have to do that again . . . with bells on.

The phone rang just as Rose was on her way out. It was Abigail to say that Pippa wanted Rosie to go to the cinema with them.

'I don't mind taking both of them, Rose. So, is it OK with you if it's OK with Rosie's uncle? We're at out-of-school club now and he's just driven into the car park.'

Rose stifled a sigh. This sort of thing would be happening all the time now. Friday had cemented the little girls' friendship even more deeply. She would never do anything to spoil it. She'd just have to live with seeing Matt out of work as well as in work.

'Yes, it's fine by me, Abigail. If Matthew agrees, tell him I'll pick up the girls from your house. I'll see him at work so we can sort out then if he wants to fetch her from here or if he wants me to drive her home.'

At least, thought Rose, as she turned into the health centre car park twenty minutes later, having to speak to Matthew about this evening's arrangements will get our first conversation since Friday out of the way quickly.

And here he is now. Rose saw the Range Rover approach the staff parking area as she began to reverse into her spot.

Her hands felt clammy on the steering wheel, her heart began to thump, pounding in her ears. It was hard to breathe, hard to concentrate . . .

Her rear bumper hit the bollard with an almighty thud.

'Oh no! I don't believe it!'

She sat still for a few seconds, before she selected first gear and inched the car forward. Then she switched off the ignition.

'Well, none of that hurt,' she muttered as she unfastened her seatbelt. 'Hopefully I've got away with it.'

Her car door opened suddenly and

Matthew leaned in. 'How on earth did you manage to do that?' he barked. Then, although his eyes remained cold, his tone gentled, 'Are you all right, Rose?'

She would have felt better if he hadn't been so close. How could she stay cool, calm and collected and treat him like a mere acquaintance? How could she act as though that kiss had never happened when his mouth was within touching distance?

She wanted to . . .

'No.' The word came out in a distressed whisper.

'You're not all right?' He inched closer.

'No . . . I mean, I'm all right . . . Just don't touch me, Matthew.'

Her words hurt. Did she dislike him so much that she couldn't bear him anywhere near?

Not dislike — distrust, whispered a voice in his head. She thinks it's a ploy, you wanting to help her — just like she thought you kissing her was a ploy.

'I have no intention of touching you, Rose.'

He withdrew and straightened up then, forcing his face into an impassive mask, he watched her experiment with a series of gentle neck movements.

He wanted to touch her. Heavens, how he wanted to take her in his arms, feel her softness against him again, run soothing fingers over her shoulders and neck.

Pippa had told him, 'Auntie Rose wasn't very well yesterday, she had a migraine.'

Reversing into the bollard must have really jarred her head.

He watched her reach across to the passenger seat and pick up her large bag, then swivel round.

He wanted to help her out of the car, take her bag. But she'd made it obvious she didn't want him near her.

Misery rooted him to the spot.

'Excuse me, Matthew,' she prompted. She couldn't trust her legs to hold her if she had to get out while he was standing so close to the car door.

He stepped back and she moved upwards slowly, testing her muscles.

'If I have suffered whiplash it's only slight,' she said. And now, perversely, she wanted him to touch her, wanted him to offer comfort.

'Perhaps you'd best ask Audrey to take a look, just in case,' he said.

Rose winced. OK, so he still thought she was out to . . . to trap him into a relationship to secure the farmhouse. But he didn't have to make it so clear that he couldn't bear to touch her.

'I'll take a couple of aspirins,' she told him, slamming the car door shut. 'And I've got some arnica tincture in my bag — I'll make a cold compress with it.'

Always an alternative remedy, he thought. But I can't think of any alternative way of coping with my feelings for her other than keeping her at arm's length, keeping things as impersonal as possible.

Happily there was one other topic of

conversation readily available to him.

'It was good of your friend Abigail, offering to take Rosie to the cinema,' he said as they walked towards the building. 'Though I think Rosie's more excited about seeing Thomas and Abigail's smallholding than going to the cinema. What sort of animals have they got?' There, that was pretty impersonal.

'Ducks, hens, cats, two dogs and a few Jacob sheep.'

'Do they breed from the sheep?' Matthew asked.

'Usually,' Rose replied. 'Luckily, though, it isn't their livelihood. They know the potential risks to a pregnant woman so they purposely decided against the flock having any lambs this year and there won't be any in spring, either.'

They had come to the side entrance — a narrow single door — and Rose tried to shrink her body so that she wouldn't brush against him.

'Abigail did tell you I'd pick up Rose and Pippa from her place?' she asked as they walked along the corridor. 'I can have Rosie home by nine at the latest if that's OK with you?'

'Were you planning on picking Pippa up anyway? I don't want to impose.'

'Yes, we arranged it when I knew I'd be working late this evening. I'm going straight from here,' Rose replied. They'd reached her treatment room now, but she didn't open the door because she didn't want Matthew to follow her in. She needed respite; it was so hard trying to treat him coolly.

'You don't usually work Monday evenings.'

'I'm going to pop home at five-thirty to see to the goats and hens, then I'm coming back to take Shirley's place at the Family Planning Clinic. I'm paying back the hours she worked for me on Friday.' Drat. Why did she have to go and mention Friday?

'So is that all right then, if I have Rosie home by nine?' she added quickly.

'Yes, now I know it isn't an

imposition, I can get to the Friends Of The Hospital meeting for seven-thirty. That means I should be home soon after nine . . . I only have to show my face for a while. But in any case, Pamela will be able to put Rosie to bed and read her a story.'

'OK, now that's settled, we'd best get on.' And, without looking at him again, Rose walked into her treatment room and closed the door firmly behind her.

That was the first hurdle over; she had shut the door on him. But now she felt bereft, as though he had abandoned her. It wasn't his fault, though — she had told him not to touch her, hadn't she? Had he wanted to, she wondered?

'Work,' she muttered, 'concentrate on work.'

Mondays were always busy but because half-term always gave children more opportunity to have accidents, Rose's morning list was longer than usual.

Two youngsters had fallen into a bramble bush whilst blackberrying, another had fallen while skateboarding, one had come off her bike, and yet another had twisted his ankle while jumping off a wall.

Rose only had time for a ten-minute break at lunch. She sat in her room and ate her sandwiches, pressing an arnica compress to her neck with her other hand. She still thought her little accident hadn't caused any damage, but she knew all too well that whiplash injuries didn't always present themselves immediately.

There was a light tap at the door and Julia popped her head in. 'Ready for the Asthma Clinic, Rose? What are you doing?' she added, walking in.

'Hopefully it's just a preventative measure.' Rose smiled at her colleague and went on to tell her about her argument with the bollard.

'I've always been useless at parking,' she added ruefully, removing the compress.

'What about the exercise session?' asked Julia as they made their way to the clinic room.

Rose had been delighted to discover that the practice had a strong policy on preventative measures within the Asthma Clinic and had a range of equipment for testing respiratory efficiency. However, she'd soon decided to introduce some yoga-related breathing exercises into the sessions as well. So far it seemed to be working well. Today would be the third exercise session.

'Doing the lion, camel and rabbit exercises will relax me, too,' Rose assured Julia.

The Asthma Clinic overran so, when she popped home, Rose only had time to milk Grizelda and settle her, along with Topsy and the hens for the night, before returning to the health centre for the family planning session.

She caught a glimpse of Matthew at his surgery door as he saw a patient out. He looked tired and fraught, as though he had the cares of the world on his shoulders. Perhaps he'd had to relate some upsetting news to his patient.

Rose longed to go to him, to ask him if talking would help, to offer comfort, love and understanding. But when he caught her glance, he gave a curt nod and quickly closed his door.

'Just as well really,' Rose muttered. 'No doubt he'd have misread my intentions anyway.'

The family planning clinic wasn't very busy. She managed to get away for seven o'clock, so when she arrived at Abigail's she was in time to share the after-cinema supper Abigail had made for the two girls.

As they helped clear the table, Pippa chatted about the film they'd seen but, as Matthew had guessed, the smallholding and the animals had made the bigger impression on Rosie.

'Abigail says if it's OK with Uncle Matt, I can come with Pippa for the . . . what is it you call them, Pippa?'

'Christmas-present-making Saturdays,' said Pippa.

'Yes, that's it,' said Rosie. 'You make wool dolls to hang on the Christmas trees, and fluffy lamb cards, don't you . . . and orange pomanders . . . and — '

'And secrets, Rosie,' hissed Pippa. 'Come over to the window to talk about it,' she added in a loud whisper.

Rose shot Abigail an enquiring look. Pippa spending all the November Saturdays before Christmas with Abigail, making cards, presents and decorations, was a tradition that had started when Hannah was alive. Rose hadn't been sure if Pippa would still want to continue it; she'd thought it might upset her, so she hadn't mentioned it.

'It was when they showed the trailer for the next film at the cinema,' Abigail said as she ran water into the washing-up bowl. 'They announced it was starting on Saturday November second. Pips said she wouldn't be able to see it then because she'd be here, making presents.

'Then,' Abigail continued quietly, 'as

soon as we got here, we showed Rosie the Jacobs. I showed her some of the wool I'd spun and said we always used some of the Jacobs' wool to make Christmassy things. That's when Pippa asked me if Rosie could come on Saturdays, too. They're bound to have sad days around Christmas, aren't they? I thought being together might help them.'

'I'm sure it will,' Rose agreed. 'I'll mention it to Matthew, see what he thinks.'

'Won't his wife have any say in it?' Abigail asked curiously.

'He isn't married, Abigail,' Rose said dully, drying the last plate over and over again. 'I got it wrong. Pamela is Matthew's aunt.'

'So why aren't you jumping over the moon?' demanded Abigail. 'It's OK for you to fancy him if he's single.' She took the plate from Rose and put it with the rest of the dried crockery.

'You've liked him right from the

word go,' she added. 'And you'd be so perfect for each other, Rose, you've got so much in common. You work together, you're both bringing up a niece on your own, the two of them are best friends, Rosie thinks the world of you and — '

'And I don't want to talk about it.' Rose interrupted her friend's flow. 'Let's just say something happened to make it so I still can't let him know how I feel.'

Tears stinging her eyes, Rose threw down the tea towel and turned to face the girls.

'Home time, you two,' she said brightly. 'I know it's school holidays but that doesn't mean you can stay up too late.'

Rose rushed them through their goodbyes and thank yous and out into the car before Abigail could ask her any more about Matthew.

★ ★ ★

226

'I will be able to come back on Saturdays, won't I?' Rosie asked anxiously as she and Pippa waved to Abigail.

'Maybe not every Saturday, Rosie. Your uncle might have other plans,' Rose replied. 'Now,' she added, 'no more talking to me while I'm driving, please.'

Shortly afterwards, Rose drew up outside Matthew's house.

'You stay in the car, Pippa, while I walk Rosie to the front door,' she said. 'I'll only be a minute.'

Although Rose had never met Pamela, it was obvious the minute the older woman opened the door that she wasn't at all well. One side of her face was swollen and her face was scrunched in pain.

'Toothache again,' she mumbled, 'I think it's another abscess or a dry socket.'

'Have you taken anything for it?' Rose asked.

'I didn't dare take my painkillers,

they knock me out. I've got to stay awake for Rosie; Matthew phoned to say he'd be late. And,' she added on a sigh as a demanding yapping came from somewhere inside the house, 'Sasha ate a twig or something when I took her into the back garden. Now she keeps being sick. I've shut her in the kitchen.

'I'm not usually so useless,' she said disgustedly. 'I just can't — '

'Poor Sasha. I'll go and love her better,' said Rosie. 'I'll be careful not to let her out,' she added, as she dashed into the house.

'She's such a good child,' said Pamela, 'but I can't think straight when my face is throbbing like this — it makes everything seem like hard work.'

'I'll take Rosie back with me to stay the night,' said Rose impulsively. 'She can bring Sasha, too. Then you can take your painkillers and go to bed.'

'That sounds like heaven,' said Pamela. 'Matthew told me how much they all enjoyed themselves at your

228

house last week. But . . . '

'It doesn't matter about Rosie's night things or clean clothes for morning, she's the same size as Pippa,' Rose continued. 'Has she got a favourite toy she takes to bed with her?'

'Plod, her elephant,' said Pamela. 'But I can't let you . . . '

'Of course you can,' Rose said firmly.

'What about letting Matthew know . . . I don't want to phone him on his mobile when it isn't an emergency.'

'I'll go to the car and write him a note while you get Rosie's elephant,' Rose told her. 'I'll let Pippa know what's happening, too. She'll be delighted.'

Rose kept a supply of scrap paper in the glove compartment; Pippa often enjoyed drawing pictures when they were on their way to somewhere.

I only hope Matthew doesn't think I'm interfering or that I have an ulterior motive — like getting him up to the house tonight when the girls are in bed, Rose thought, smiling ruefully at

Pippa's excitement as she worked out how to word the note.

If I tell him I'll take the girls to out-of-school club in the morning and that I'll leave Sasha in the kitchen, and where the back door key will be so he can collect her, that should do it. It'll be obvious then that I'm not expecting him to come round while I'm there.

As for Rosie wanting to go to Abigail's for the next few Saturdays, she would have to try to find the right moment to mention that.

★ ★ ★

How right I was not to let her know how I feel, thought Matthew, when he read Rose's note an hour or so later. She'd never have believed I love her and want her for herself and not for helping out with Rosie like she's done this evening. And it's clear she doesn't want me at the house while she's there . . .

He crumpled the paper into a tight

hard ball and flung it into the wastepaper bin, only to have to go and retrieve it and straighten it out to get Rose's phone number.

Drawing in deep breaths in an effort to force himself into a cool and collected frame of mind, he lifted the telephone and jabbed the buttons.

Rose sounded breathless and a bit giggly when she replied to his curt: 'It's Matthew.'

'I don't know if Sasha did it all on her own or whether the girls helped her,' she laughed, 'but whichever it was, she joined them in the bath, which she thoroughly enjoyed, but she doesn't like being dried. So now I'm wet, too.'

Matthew's mouth dried as a vision of Rose, damp, crumpled, pink and warm floated into his mind.

'The girls are in bed but I haven't tucked them in and kissed them goodnight yet,' Rose continued. 'I'll give . . .'

He missed the rest of what she was saying. He was wishing he could be there to share in the fun, to be part of it. They'd tuck the girls up, kiss them goodnight and go downstairs and sit in front of the fire together . . . on the fluffy hearthrug maybe . . . and then . . .

'Matthew?'

'Mmm, sorry, what were you saying?'

'I said I'll give Rosie a kiss for you.'

'Yes, OK, thank you.'

'You aren't annoyed about me bringing her here, are you?' she ventured. 'Pamela was in so much pain it just seemed the best thing to do . . . and . . .'

'I'm not annoyed, of course I'm not. I'm very grateful. You must let me repay you somehow . . . take Pippa out for the day or something.'

His tone . . . his words . . . were cold . . . aloof . . .

Rose felt sad and furious at the same time.

But he had given her a chance to mention Rosie spending some Saturdays at Abigail's.

'There is something you can do,

Matthew . . . ' and Rose went on to tell him about the present-making tradition. 'So, if you'll let Rosie go with Pippa, I think it might help both of them through what's sure to be a traumatic time.'

'I must admit I'm dreading Christmas,' he acknowledged. 'You must be, too, Rose. Anything that might help is more than all right by me. But you'll have to let me take my turn at ferrying Rosie and Pippa to Abigail's and back.'

Rose panicked then.

'We'll have to work out a convenient picking up and dropping off spot for us at this end,' she said. 'Maybe by the gate at the bottom of the hill up to the farmhouse.'

Matthew's pain at Rose's suggestion was almost a tangible thing.

She couldn't have made it clearer that I wouldn't be welcome in her home, he thought.

There didn't seem anything left to say then — except to wish her goodnight.

Rose didn't see much of Matthew over the next few days. On Thursday he was called out to an emergency just before the Mother and Baby Clinic so, once again, Rose worked with Audrey Gordon.

'November tomorrow.' Audrey sighed as they tidied up at the end of the session. 'What's that saying about it . . . 'No shade no shine, no fruits no flowers, no leaves no birds, November.' They ought to add 'No rest for doctors' to that. It's the month for coughs and colds and bronchitis and flu.'

'My list of patients wanting flu vaccinations is horrendous,' Rose agreed. 'But hopefully, with so many taking that precaution, you might get off lighter than you think.'

'Hope springs eternal,' said Audrey, heading back to her office with a laugh.

★   ★   ★

Audrey Gordon's prophecy about November came true. Not only was there a flu epidemic, but a virulent tummy bug hit the area too.

All three doctors and the practice nurses were run off their feet. Coffee breaks and lunch breaks ceased to exist. The only contact Rose had with Matthew was if he phoned through to her treatment room to ask if she could set up some test or other.

The weather was appalling, too. Whenever they met at the bottom of the hill to pick up and drop off Rosie or Pippa, it was done in a rush to prevent a soaking. There was never any time for chat.

There seemed to be an impenetrable barrier between them.

Rose knew life had to go on, but there was a cold empty space in her chest where her heart had once been, and when Pippa's counsellor, Josh, arrived at the farmhouse unexpectedly one Sunday, Rose found herself telling him about Matthew.

Even though there was a generation gap — Josh was due for retirement

— Rose knew he hadn't earned his nickname of 'Gentle Giant' just because of his size. She knew he would understand . . .

'I'm sure nobody could ever think you were devious enough to pretend to have feelings to try to trap him into a commitment,' Josh said, when Rose finished talking. 'Besides, you said it looks as if Richard's business has been sold. As soon as that's signed, sealed and settled, you could find a way of telling Matthew.'

'Mmm, perhaps,' Rose agreed doubtfully. 'But that doesn't take away the fact that he thought I was trying to trap him.'

Josh rubbed his bald head with one huge hand.

'You don't know that for sure. That's just your interpretation of the way you said he looked at you. And I know it's not much consolation at the moment, but if you and Matthew are meant to be together, it will happen in time.'

'Matthew and Auntie Rose together

where?' Pippa bounded into the room to hear Josh's last few words.

'I'm starving,' she added, without waiting for a reply. 'Please may I have an apple? Two, maybe, 'cos Topsy and Grizelda are hungry, too.'

'She's doing marvellously, Rose,' said Josh as Pippa dashed out again.

'Yes, she is.' Rose smiled. 'That's all that should matter really. I was a bit worried about the present-making sessions with Abigail. I thought the memories might upset her. But so far . . . ' She held up crossed fingers. ' . . . Pippa's enjoying them more than ever. Probably because Rosie is sharing them with her. And next Saturday's the last one.'

Josh left soon afterwards but his visit had cheered Rose up a bit.

* * *

Perhaps it was because she felt more cheerful that the following week seemed to fly past.

237

The weather changed on Saturday. It was a grey, still morning, but a feeble sun was trying to break through the purple mist shrouding the moors and the air was filled with the delicious scent of fallen leaves.

It was Rose's turn to take Pippa and Rosie to Abigail's. Matthew was waiting by the farm gate at the bottom of the hill and Rose's heart skipped a beat as she drew up and watched him open it.

He was wearing a plaid padded shirt and cord trousers, and looked devastatingly handsome, and she swallowed hard as her eyes followed his movements.

She drove through the gate and he closed it, and Rosie clambered out of his Range Rover and skipped over to Rose's car, her face bright with excitement.

Matthew settled his niece into the back seat then closed the door and leaned towards Rose's open window. Rose had turned her head to talk to Rosie and Pippa, her hair swinging softly as she moved. He could smell her perfume and, as she turned her head back, he caught the tail end of the smile she'd bestowed on the girls.

'I'll pick them up from Abigail's around six so we should be here between six-thirty and seven,' he said abruptly.

Rose nodded. 'Fine. I'll be waiting.'

Sighing, Matthew watched her drive off.

★   ★   ★

When she returned from Abigail's, Rose spent the rest of the day gardening. She pulled up annuals, cut down perennials, trimmed bushes, swept up leaves, and burned everything on a bonfire. She was hot, messy and tired — and looking forward to a long soak in a bath perfumed with geranium and grapefruit oil, when the phone rang.

It was Pippa. 'Abigail says Matthew's got to go somewhere, so will you come and fetch us? I can't stop to chat,

Auntie Rose, 'cos we're baking.'

As she put the phone down, a frown pleated Rose's brow. Pippa had sounded . . . worried . . . ?

No, she mused, not worried, a bit tense. Well, the sooner I get to Abigail's, the sooner I'll know. Goodbye, long soak, hello, brisk shower!

Just as Rose parked her car in the smallholding's yard, Matthew's Range Rover came down the drive. He must have finished whatever he had to do sooner than he expected, thought Rose, and, secretly glad that she would have a couple of minutes alone with him, she waited for him to park.

'So, what are you doing here, Rose?' he asked as soon as he was out of the Range Rover.

'Abigail said you had to go somewhere — she seemed to think you wouldn't be able to pick up the girls,' she replied.

Wherever he's been he looks fantastic, she thought, noting his pale-coloured crew neck sweater and dark chinos.

'But I haven't spoken to Abigail,' he said. 'Where could she have got that idea from?'

Rose shrugged. 'I've got a feeling something's going on,' she told him. 'I thought Pippa sounded strange when she phoned and gave me the message. I didn't actually speak to Abigail.'

She smiled. 'Well, there's only one way to find out. Come on, we'll go in the back way.'

Neither spoke as they walked round to the back of the house.

The sound of their feet scrunching on the pebbles heralded their arrival and the door opened before they reached it. Pippa and Rosie stood there laughing.

'We've got a surprise for you!' Pippa announced in delight. 'Welcome to the Stir-day party.'

From behind her, Rose heard Matthew stifle a laugh. 'We've been set up!' he said.

'It was because we wanted you both to be here for the Stir-day party,' said

Pippa. 'Come on, come into the kitchen and you'll see what we mean.'

Abigail was at the kitchen table using a wooden spoon to stir something in a huge bowl. All around her were smaller bowls containing dried fruit, sugar, nuts, apple, spices, flour . . .

'It was nothing to do with me,' she said, looking up from her task to smile at Rose and Matthew. 'They didn't tell me how they'd plotted to get you both here until ten minutes ago.'

'Here for Stir-day. It means we all take it in turns to stir the Christmas pudding mixture and make a wish,' said Rosie. 'Thomas and Aidan will stir, too. Thomas has gone to look for charms and coins and special things to put in the pudding . . .'

'Thomas has found them,' Thomas announced as he walked into the room, holding clenched fists in front of his chest.

' . . . and Aidan had to go and see a sick pig but he should be back soon,' Rosie finished what she'd been saying.

'And it will be a party 'cos we've baked cinnamon buns and angel biscuits and made a fruit punch.' Pippa laughed. 'We might put up the Christmas tree, too, 'cos we've made advent calendars to hang on it and advent begins tomorrow.'

'We can stay for the party, can't we, Uncle Matt?' Rosie asked anxiously. 'We weren't doing anything tonight, were we?'

Rose waited as anxiously as Rosie for Matthew's answer. She wanted him to stay, wanted this unexpected time with him. Abigail's house was 'neutral territory' and the relaxed party atmosphere might help break down the barriers between them.

When Matthew screwed his face into an exaggerated thinking expression, she let out a silent sigh of relief. He was going to stay.

Rosie had recognised her uncle's expression, too.

'It's going to be all right, Pips,' she yelled. 'Let's all of us give three cheers for Uncle Matt.'

Aidan arrived at the end of the cheering session. After Rose had introduced him to Matthew, Aidan turned to her and enveloped her in a huge hug.

Watching, Matthew felt a cold, lonely despair creep through every inch of his body. And when the other man kissed Rose firmly on the mouth, Matthew wanted to hit him. But the feeling abated quickly when Aidan spoke.

'Rose played a part in helping me find the girl of my dreams,' he announced to everyone in general. 'Linda and I met at the garden centre when I was helping Rose one day.'

'Come on — enough chat! There's a pudding waiting to be stirred,' said Abigail, waving the wooden spoon around.

'And wishes to make,' said Pippa.

She grabbed Rosie's hand and, giggling, the two little girls walked over to stand by Abigail and Thomas.

'We know you shouldn't tell what you wish,' said Pippa as she took the spoon from her godmother, 'but me and Rosie have decided to say part of our wish out loud and we want Auntie Rose and Uncle Matthew to listen carefully.'

Matthew stepped closer to Rose. 'Uh-oh, something's going on,' he murmured into her ear.

Rose chuckled . . . and waited . . .

'We wish,' chanted the girls together, 'that we could spend Christmas Day and Boxing Day together.'

'And now we'll make our other wish but that one's a secret one,' said Rosie.

'We can make one wish come true,' Rose said quietly, looking up at Matthew with a smile that turned his legs to jelly. 'You, Rosie and Pamela could come to the farmhouse for Christmas Day. Abigail, Thomas and Aidan are coming and I think Lucy and Harry are as well. And maybe I could take the girls out for the day on Boxing Day.'

'No,' said Matthew, and Rose felt her happiness ooze away. 'I mean no, don't take them out on Boxing Day. If . . . '

He raised his voice so Rosie and Pippa could hear. 'If we are coming to you on Christmas Day, Rose, you and Pippa must come to us on Boxing Day.'

Pippa and Rosie hugged each other in delight then demanded that everyone else lined up to take their turn at stirring and wishing.

'I'd better warn you,' Rose told Matthew as they watched Aidan stir the pudding, 'it's a family tradition that all Christmas presents are hand-made.'

The rest of the evening passed in a happy haze for Rose. Granted, this party and the arrangements for Christmas were for their nieces' sakes, but the bond between her and Matthew was forming again.

The kiss under the mistletoe — engineered by the giggling girls, aided and abetted by Abigail — was more, much more, than the obligatory peck on the cheek. It was warm and gentle and tender; Rose was sure she sensed in Matthew the same yearnings that filled her heart, her mind and her soul. She was equally sure he was as reluctant to end the kiss as she was.

If only he could accept that her feelings for him were because he was who he was — and not for any other reason . . .

Wishes Come True

To Pippa's delight, there was a slight scattering of hailstones on the morning of Christmas Day. 'So it's almost a white Christmas,' she giggled as she sat on Rose's bed to open the presents in her stocking.

'I'm glad it hasn't snowed,' said Rose. 'What if we'd been snowed in? Our visitors wouldn't have been able to get to us.'

She was so looking forward to Matthew and Rosie coming. And everyone else, too, she added as she moved aside a pile of discarded wrapping paper to get out of bed.

Once they'd fed the goats and hens — Pippa insisted on giving them a special breakfast — the morning passed in a flurry of preparation and excitement.

Matthew and Rosie arrived earlier

than expected. Rosie was carrying a bag in the shape of a Christmas stocking.

'It's full of presents for everyone,' she said, hugging Rose and laughing as Sasha joined in.

'I hope you don't mind us getting here so soon,' said Matthew as Pippa and Rosie ran off to put the presents under the tree. 'Rosie just couldn't wait any longer.

'We've just dropped Pamela off at church — I'll pick her up after the service.'

Rose's heart skipped a beat as she welcomed him with a hug and a kiss. It was just a friendly kiss, but that didn't stop her senses from whirling as she inhaled his scent, felt the strength of his shoulders beneath his soft cashmere sweater, heard the beating of his heart.

'I don't mind at all,' she assured him huskily. 'I can put you to work. How about lighting the lounge fire for me?'

Memories of the day he and Rose had knelt together on the hearthrug making toast filled Matthew's mind as he set light to the ready-laid fire.

Memories of their first kiss mingled with the memory of the one under the mistletoe . . . and the latest one just a few minutes ago.

But Rosie and Pippa were demanding his attention; he reminded himself sternly that he and Rose were doing this for the girls.

And once everyone else arrived, there was no time to think of what might have been as they all joined in with one party game after another — most of them organised by Aidan.

Throughout the noisy, happy day, though, Matthew couldn't prevent his gaze from lingering on Rose whenever she was near him.

Abigail was delighted when Rose was the one to find the silver ring in her portion of Christmas pudding.

'It means you'll be married within a year,' she said, slanting a quick glance Matthew's way.

'I've got the button,' sighed Aidan. 'That means I'll be a bachelor for ever.'

Rosie and Pippa each found a silver coin in their portions; Thomas winked at Rose as they exclaimed in delight.

The only sad moment was the one before 'present-opening time'. Pippa and Rosie suddenly became quiet and thoughtful. Matthew moved close to Rose.

'Is this the moment the memories start to hurt them?' he said quietly.

'Could be,' Rose whispered, blinking away her tears. 'But maybe I can find something to help them through it. Give it a few minutes, Matt, then come upstairs.'

Rose walked over to crouch down by the little girls who were sitting next to Lucy on the settee with Sasha sprawled out over their legs.

'I think maybe we should go up to my bedroom and tidy ourselves before we open the presents,' she suggested, lifting up the puppy and passing her to Lucy.

As Rose had hoped, when she and the girls had combed their hair, Pippa's hand wandered to the pretty box containing the gemstones and crystals.

'Perhaps you and Rosie would like to choose a helping stone?' Rose suggested gently.

'You knew, didn't you?' asked Pippa, stroking her stone. 'You knew Rosie and I were feeling sad.'

Rose nodded and hugged them both to her.

'We've been trying to stay brave,' said Pippa, 'and you've made a lovely Christmas Day for us, but . . .'

'But we've never had a Christmas without our mummies or daddies before,' gulped Rosie.

'I miss Pippa's mummy and daddy, too,' said Rose, 'and Uncle Matthew misses yours, Rosie.'

'I do,' said Matthew, walking into the room. 'And I think I need a big hug, too,' he added gruffly.

'We all do,' agreed Pippa. 'We'll all hug each other all at once, 'cos we're sort of like a family now.'

I wish, thought Rose.

She couldn't look at Matthew; she was scared the yearning would show in her eyes.

And, once again, Matthew thought longingly of what might have been.

'We're better now, aren't we, Rosie?' said Pippa.

'Yes.' Rosie wriggled free and smiled up at Matthew and Rose. 'Let's go downstairs so we can all open our presents.'

The girls hurried out of the room, leaving Matthew and Rose alone.

Matthew turned Rose towards him and kissed her ... hard and briefly on the lips, before he followed the girls.

Rose took the silver ring from the pudding out of her pocket and dropped it into the box with the gemstones. Maybe one of the stones would make her wish come true. Then, smiling at her whimsical thought, she made her way downstairs.

The presents varied from funny little ornaments made from conkers and acorns to hand-knitted scarves and hats and — from Matthew to Rose — a beautiful rose carved out of wood.

'I cheated,' Matthew admitted, smiling as Rose, blushing prettily, thanked him. 'I didn't make it myself.'

'I broke the rule slightly as well,' said Aidan, who had given everyone the same thing — a ticket to a New Year's Eve barn party at a local farm. 'But I did make the envelopes.'

When all the presents had been opened, Rose turned the radio on and they listened to Christmas songs while chestnuts roasted on the fire. Sasha made everyone laugh by yapping every time a chestnut popped open.

The day drew to a close and Pippa announced that their first Christmas at the farmhouse had been magic and she hoped everyone would come again next year.

'And your baby, of course, Abigail,' she added, rubbing her godmother's tummy.

'From the amount of kicking, I think

the baby enjoyed today, too,' laughed Abigail.

As Rose said goodbye to Matthew, she managed to murmur to him that Richard's business had been sold.

'So it's safe to say that this Christmas is the first of many here.'

There. At least now, if she let her love show in an unguarded moment, he'd know that she didn't need him to secure the farmhouse for her.

However, to Rose's dismay, although Boxing Day at Matthew's was enjoyable, he seemed to hold himself aloof from her.

At the health centre, too — open mornings only during the days up to New Year — Matthew reverted to treating her politely and coolly.

It was the only way he could cope, he told himself, whenever he saw the hurt, bewildered expression in Rose's eyes. Pippa's words: 'We're sort of like a family now', had brought home once again how it would look to Rose if he told her how he felt.

If he told her that more than anything he wanted them to be a family, she'd think it was only for Rosie's sake.

★ ★ ★

New Year's Eve was crisply cold and frosty, the sky was fathomless dark velvet, the stars twinkled and the moon shone brightly. It couldn't have been a better evening for the barn dance, Rose thought.

The farm where the barn dance was being held was at the end of a long and bumpy track and Rose lost count of the cattle grids they had to drive over.

'I'm glad you offered to bring us, Matthew,' she said. 'I'm not sure my car would have stood up to this.'

They were almost the first words she'd spoken since greeting him when he'd picked them up. Until now, she hadn't been able to think of anything to say; she'd spent the entire journey torturing herself by watching his hands on the steering wheel, or the movement of his thigh when he changed gear.

'That's OK. The girls wanted to be together,' he replied tersely.

'Rosie and I are really, really excited,' Pippa trilled from the back seat. 'We've never been to a barn party before. I wonder where all the sheep are? There aren't any in the fields or on the hills. We've been looking.'

'It's probably a dairy farm,' Rose said. 'I think cows spend winter inside in shippons.'

'It looks as if half the county is here,' Matthew said as he drew to a halt in a field already packed with parked cars. 'It's as well Pamela didn't want to come — she isn't keen on crowds.'

'Sounds like there's a live band, too,' Rose observed when she opened the vehicle's door and the sound of a campfire cowboy song reached them.

'No running off yet,' she ordered Pippa and Rosie, waiting while Matthew secured some newspaper across the car windscreen to save it freezing later. 'We don't want you to start the evening by losing us.'

'Thomas and Abigail are here,' said Pippa as they made their way across the field. 'Look, that's their car. I know it's theirs 'cos I remember the number.'

When they arrived at the farmyard gates, it was clear that the event was well organised. They'd already passed a First Aid ambulance van and when they handed their tickets to the plump, jolly-looking man at the gate, he said, 'Take the little misses to one of the scarecrows — you'll see a dozen or so of them — they're here to look after the children.

'It's OK,' he added quietly to Rose and Matthew. 'It's my farm, I'm Reg Thornton. The scarecrow helpers are all from the local day nurseries and kiddies' clubs.'

'Do you think they're real scarecrows come to life?' asked Rosie, her eyes big and round with excitement as they walked into the farmyard.

'Probably.' Matthew laughed as he

ruffled his niece's hair.

Watching him, Rose's heart flipped in the way it so often did when Matthew was near.

She looked away quickly and inhaled deeply, breathing in the faint aroma of farmyard, woodsmoke and charcoal from the barbecues that floated on the freshness of a cold winter's evening.

And now I'll think of Matthew every time I smell barbecue smoke, she thought with a sigh of helplessness.

A teenage girl dressed as a scarecrow appeared in front of them.

'Hi, I'm Muddy Maddie,' she said, smiling down at Pippa and Rosie. She pointed to a smaller outbuilding. 'There's a puppet show in there and there'll be dancing when it's finished.'

She looked up at Matthew. 'I'll keep an eye on your girls if you want to go and get a drink or have a dance — that's in the big barn attached to the house. We'll come and find you when it's time for the food.'

Pippa and Rose grinned at each other.

'Go on, Auntie Rose — you go and dance with Matthew and Rosie and I will go with Muddy Maddie,' she giggled.

The girls hurried off, and although people swirled around them, Rose suddenly felt as if she and Matthew were alone inside an invisible circle of electricity.

Looking down at her, Matthew longed to pull her into his arms, ached for the warmth of her body against his, wanted the touch of her fingers . . .

'There you are! We've been looking for you for ages.' Abigail's voice broke them from the spell. 'Thomas grabbed a couple of glasses of hot spiced fruit punch for you in case it ran out — he's waiting just inside the barn.'

She looked from one to the other of them. 'I don't know why you're looking so puzzled to see me. We did arrange to meet up around seven o'clock.'

'I . . . er . . . I'm just amazed you managed to find us in this crush,' said Rose.

'It was easy. You two were standing like stuffed dummies while everyone else passed by you. Come on, Rose — Thomas wants to dance and it'll have to be with you because my bump would get in the way.'

Abigail linked one hand through Matthew's arm and the other through Rose's and led them towards the barn. They found Thomas and he handed them their drinks.

'Aidan and Linda are somewhere around,' he told them, 'but Lucy and Harry decided they wouldn't come.'

It was hard to make themselves heard over the music, so they stood and watched the dancers for a while. Then Thomas took Rose's half-finished drink from her, passed it to Abigail to hold and led Rose into the middle of the dance area.

Forty minutes later, pink and breathless, Rose flopped down next to Abigail on one of the bundles of straw that had been placed against the barn walls as seating. The live band had stopped playing and quieter music came from a CD player.

'Thomas has gone to wait in the queue for food. I said we'd join him in a few minutes,' Rose told her friend.

'Aidan's been called out,' said Abigail. 'It's a shame when coming here was his idea, but he didn't think he'd be long.'

Rose didn't comment; her eyes were on the dancing couples.

'He's dancing with Linda,' Abigail said.

Rose turned to her, startled. 'Who is?'

'Come off it, Rose, don't pretend you weren't looking for Matthew.'

Rose felt herself flushing, then she gave a shaky laugh and shrugged.

'Ridiculous, isn't it? After Stephen, I swore I would never fall in love again, and now here I am like a teenager suffering from unrequited love.'

'I'm not so sure it is unrequited. I've seen the way Matthew looks at you.'

Rose pulled at a piece of straw, easing

it from the bundle.

'There was one glorious moment when I was sure he felt the same way as I do,' she said quietly. 'But the moment ended almost before it had started. Anyway,' she added, 'I'll get over him. It's just — it's so hard when Pippa and Rosie are best friends and I have to see him all the time.'

★ ★ ★

Muddy Maddie appeared in the doorway with Pippa and Rosie just then, and Rose stood up to wave to them.

'Why don't you take them to join Thomas in the queue?' Abigail suggested. 'I wouldn't be able to stand for so long — I'll wait here and tell Matthew where you are.'

The food was being cooked over three separate barbecues and Thomas was standing in the queue nearest the farmyard gates.

As Rose shepherded the little girls through the crowd towards him, they told her all about the puppet show and the dancing.

'It sounds like fun,' Rose remarked, smiling down at the two happy little faces.

'It was — but I'm really hungry now,' said Rosie. 'Do you think they'll have ketchup?'

Rose laughed as they joined Thomas in the queue.

'Yes, I'm sure they'll . . . '

She broke off as the sound of raucous laughter, wolf-whistles, yells, thuds and bangs filled the air. This was followed by catcalls and then suddenly fireworks were whizzing everywhere. A few people screamed in fright.

There was a horrendous bellowing noise — then came a man's voice, loud and urgent . . .

'The bull's loose! Everybody stand back! Stand back — clear a path!'

Rose grabbed Pippa and Rosie but before she could move, Maddie appeared and snatched them away from her.

'I'll get them round the back and into

the house!' she yelled, dragging the girls along with her through the open farmyard gates.

'Stand back, everybody stand back against the walls!'

Half a dozen men tried to control the swirling, yelling throng, pushing and pulling them in an effort to clear the centre of the yard.

Rose had been shoved towards the big barn and was trying to stem the hysteria of those standing nearest to her.

She caught sight of Matthew's back view as he stood in the barn entrance, his arms outstretched, and she guessed he was preventing anyone from rushing out.

The bull — tossing his huge head from side to side and roaring with rage and fear — came careering through the farmyard from the far end.

Suddenly a toddler wandered into the bull's path . . .

Without stopping to think, Rose sprang forward.

As she brought the child down with a rugby tackle and threw herself on top of him, she saw a blurred vision of two pairs of feet land in front of her.

Over the pounding sound of the bull's hooves, she heard a firm, authoritative voice: 'Steady, Angus, steady there, boy.'

And another voice that sounded like Matthew's . . .

When the pounding noise stopped, she felt hands pulling her sideways, then lifting her up, and saw another pair of hands reaching for the toddler . . .

She raised her head to see Reg Thornton standing in front of the bull, soothing it with big hands and gentle voice.

Matthew was standing at one side of the bull's huge head, pushing a hooked stick through the ring on the its nose towards Thomas who stood at the other side of the animal.

Then a stocky young man tapped Matthew on the shoulder. Matthew moved away and before Rose had time to blink, he was there in front of her, taking her into his arms, holding her close, rubbing his forehead against hers.

'Rose . . . '

'The girls are all right,' she gasped. 'Maddie got them away. She said she was taking them into the house.'

'It's you I'm worried about, Rose. Don't you ever, ever do anything like that again.' His voice broke and Rose was almost sure he was trembling slightly as he held her.

'You leapt in front of the bull, too,' she said.

'I'd just made sure Abigail wasn't getting crushed, then I stepped out of the barn and there you were — throwing yourself at that little boy! My heart nearly stopped! I thought you'd be trampled to death . . . and the thought of losing you . . . ' She felt his arms tighten around her. 'Are you all right? Are you hurting anywhere?'

'Everywhere,' she murmured. 'Keep holding me, Matt.'

'I can't, my love, I can't. There'll be people with injuries, people in shock. I need to help get them to the ambulance.'

This brought her abruptly to her senses.

'Of course. I'll help, too,' she said, wriggling out of his arms.

She saw Thomas, the farmer and two other men leading the bull back through the farmyard.

'There are quite a few First Aid attendants around,' he told her. 'You go and find Abigail and ask her to go and tell the girls everything's OK before you do anything out here.'

It was only a few yards to the barn but people kept stopping Rose to ask her if she was all right or to tell her how brave she'd been. At last, though, she managed to walk into the barn and, seeing Abigail sitting on one of the bundles of straw, hurried over to her.

'Abi?' she queried, noticing the way her friend was supporting her bump. 'Are you . . . ?'

'I thought you'd never get here.' Abigail smiled, but Rose observed the slightly worried look in her eyes. 'I was going to ask you to go and fetch Thomas, but I think . . . Rose, I think you'd better help me into the house and then phone the midwife . . . or perhaps an ambulance would be better.'

'I'll phone both,' Rose said. 'Come on — inside with you.'

Her heart thumping wildly, she helped Abigail to her feet and guided her out of the barn towards the house.

★　★　★

Twenty minutes later, Thomas dashed into the farmhouse kitchen.

'The lad you sent to fetch me has gone to fetch Matthew,' he said as he hurried over to Abigail who was half-lying and half-sitting on a large wooden table with towels and sheets underneath her.

Rose, with a sheet wrapped sari-style over her clothes, smiled over at

Thomas. 'Come and see the baby's head,' she told him, sounding far more sanguine than she felt. 'Then take your jacket off and go and scrub your hands,' she added.

The door opened and Rose glanced up, hoping to see Matthew, but it was the farmer's wife carrying a drawer.

'I've lined it with a sheepskin rug and sheets and I'll fill some hot water bottles,' she said. 'It's not much of a cot, but it'll do if the babe arrives before the ambulance gets here. It's clean and it'll be warm and cosy. Pippa and Rosie are by the fire in the sitting-room — Maddie's reading to them.'

Then Matthew arrived and Rose heaved a silent sigh of relief. She was an experienced nurse and she would have been able to cope with the arrival of a baby without him, but she was glad of his steadying, calming presence.

Matthew didn't waste time talking. He pulled his sweater off and rolled his shirtsleeves up as he walked over to the sink to wash his hands.

'How's she doing?' he asked.

'I'd better be doing OK because this baby won't wait much longer,' Abigail said between panting.

Matthew examined her swiftly, then looked up with a smile. 'Everything's fine,' he assured her. 'You've done really well.'

Glancing at Thomas, he raised his eyebrows. 'Do you want to see your son or daughter come into the world?'

As Thomas swallowed and nodded, Rose and Matthew stepped back and Rose took Matthew's hand and held it tightly.

A moment or two later, the quietness in the warm kitchen was broken by the sound of a new baby's cry.

'It's a girl,' Thomas said gruffly.

Tears filled Rose's eyes and she squeezed Matthew's hand even more tightly.

Next second, she felt his soft kiss on her cheek.

'I love you,' he whispered before he stepped forward to check the baby.

'Is she — is she all right?' Abigail asked anxiously.

'She's six weeks early, Matthew,' Thomas said hurriedly. 'Is — is she . . . will she . . . ?'

'Relax.' Matthew spoke huskily as he placed the squalling baby in Abigail's arms. 'She's perfect and seems to be quite a good weight, though I expect she'll have to stay in the prem unit for a day or so.'

Rose allowed Thomas and Abigail a couple of minutes with the baby, then went to have a look.

'She's beautiful,' she said, gently kissing the baby's head.

'Just like her mum,' said Thomas, a wide grin on his face as he stroked Abigail's damp hair back from her forehead.

There was so much love in the look which passed between Abigail and Thomas that a lump formed in Rose's throat and she had to look away.

And as she did, her eyes met Matthew's . . .

The midwife arrived at that point.

'Seems like I've missed the best part,' she said. 'The ambulance is here, Abigail, but I'll just take a quick look at you before you go. I told you I didn't think you'd go your full time, didn't I?'

She paused to admire the baby for a moment or two.

'Lovely — just beautiful,' she cooed. 'I don't know what you were thinking of, partying in your condition, though,' she added with a smile.

'It wasn't the partying,' Abigail protested. 'It was that big bad bull getting loose that scared you, wasn't it, poppet?' she crooned to the baby.

'It didn't get loose,' Thomas said grimly. 'Some lunatics got on to the land at the side of the farm, broke the padlock off the shippon door and let Angus out. The police got two of them.'

His tone softened as he looked down at his new daughter. 'But that's an episode best forgotten for the moment.'

'Right, everyone out while I examine Abigail,' the midwife ordered.

'I'll phone you tomorrow, Rose,' Abigail promised. 'And has anyone phoned Mum?' she added.

Rose laughed. 'There wasn't time. You can phone her yourself when you get to hospital.'

Smiling, Rose and Matthew left the kitchen.

Matthew put his arm around Rose's shoulders and they made their way to the sitting-room to give their nieces the news.

On their way home, Pippa asked if Rosie could stay the night.

'But we'll have to call in at our house first and fetch Sasha and Plod, Uncle Matt,' Rosie said.

Rose agreed without feeling the need to consult with Matthew.

'You're staying, too, aren't you?' she said quietly. 'The spare room's made up.'

'Nothing would keep me away,' Matthew replied.

* ★ ★

The two girls were far too excited to go to bed straight away and it was eleven-thirty before Matthew and Rose managed to get them settled down to sleep.

Finally, with the fire crackling in the grate, side lamps casting a soft glow and perfumed candles scenting the air, Rose and Matthew sat close together on the sofa and put right all the mistaken ideas they'd had about each other.

'You know,' he murmured, 'traumatic though it was, I can't help feeling grateful to those idiot louts who let the bull out.'

'And to Abigail for having the baby early,' Rose put in. 'If that hadn't happened, you might not have told me you loved me — '

'I do,' said Matthew, dropping a kiss on her nose. 'I love you with all my heart and soul.'

'Mmm, just the way I love you.' Rose snuggled closer. 'You know, Matt, even

275

without those louts we'd have got here eventually. Josh was right when he said that if you and I were meant to be together it would happen in time.'

'We *are* meant to be together,' he assured her as the clock began to strike midnight. 'This year . . . '

He kissed her hair, her eyebrows, her eyes, the tip of her nose, her cheeks, her ears, her chin . . .

' . . . and,' he murmured against her lips as the last chime of the old year struck, 'the New Year and all the following years, too. Because,' he said, lifting his face away, 'you are going to marry me, aren't you?'

Before Rose could answer, two little girls and a bundle of fur erupted into the room and leapt on to them.

'Hooray!' two little voices cheered.

'Wha — ? Pippa! Rosie, what . . . ?'

'Sasha woke us up and we sneaked down and we heard what you were saying,' said Pippa.

'Our second wish we made at the Stir-up party was for you to get married,' shrieked Rosie. 'And Pippa and I will be proper sisters and we'll have to come and live here, Uncle Matt, 'cos that's what we wished, too, and anyway, there's no room in our garden for Topsy and Grizelda and the hens.'

'Rosie, hush, you . . . ' Matthew began, but . . .

'Oh, Sasha!' Pippa cried and they all turned to look.

The puppy was so excited by the noise that she'd made a huge puddle on the rug.

Matthew groaned but Rose laughed, pushing the little girls off her and picking up the puppy.

'I'll take her into the garden and you can make us all a drink of cocoa,' she told Matthew.

'And a saucer of warm milk for Sasha,' said Rosie.

'I'm not sure that she deserves a treat like warm milk,' growled Matthew.

Once all the mopping up had been taken care of, Pippa and Rosie continued to make plans while they drank their cocoa and Rose, snuggled close against Matthew on the settee, listened in contentment.

'There's only one thing wrong.' Matthew interrupted the girls' chatter. 'Rose hasn't said she'll marry me yet.'

Pippa and Rosie looked horrified.

'Oh, Auntie Rose!' Pippa wailed.

Rose laughed softly.

'Oh, all right then. I, Rose Winter, do promise to take you, Matthew Knight —— '

'Hey, that's funny, isn't it, Rosie?' Pippa giggled. 'Rose Winter and Matthew Knight. We'll be a happy 'winter night' family. See?'

Rose smiled tenderly at Matthew.

'A very happy family. And our winter night will last for ever.'

Matthew nodded. 'Winter and Knight. An ideal complementary therapy.'

We do hope that you have enjoyed reading this large print book.

Did you know that all of our titles are available for purchase?

We publish a wide range of high quality large print books including:
Romances, Mysteries, Classics
General Fiction
Non Fiction and Westerns

Special interest titles available in large print are:
The Little Oxford Dictionary
Music Book, Song Book
Hymn Book, Service Book

Also available from us courtesy of Oxford University Press:
Young Readers' Dictionary
(large print edition)
Young Readers' Thesaurus
(large print edition)

For further information or a free brochure, please contact us at:
Ulverscroft Large Print Books Ltd.,
The Green, Bradgate Road, Anstey,
Leicester, LE7 7FU, England.
Tel: (00 44) 0116 236 4325
Fax: (00 44) 0116 234 0205

Other titles in the
Linford Romance Library:

REBECCA'S REVENGE

Valerie Holmes

Rebecca Hind's life is thrown into turmoil when her brother mysteriously disappears and she cannot keep up rent payments for their humble cottage. Help is offered by Mr Paignton of Gorebeck Lodge, although Rebecca is reluctant to leave with him and his mysterious companion. However, faced with little choice and determined to survive, Rebecca takes the offered position at the Lodge — and enters a strange world where she finds hate and love living side by side . . .

HIDDEN PLACES

Chrissie Loveday

Young widow Lauren and her son Scott have emigrated to New Zealand, where they inherit an unusual home set in a thermal park. Lauren keeps the park running smoothly for tourists, but struggles with the huge task. Desperate for help, her advertisement for assistance is answered by hunky Travis, and she believes her problems are solved. But there are major troubles ahead and important decisions to be made. Both love and deception will play a part in her dramatic new life.

THE RESTLESS HEART

Kate Allan

Isabella Oakley is travelling to her relations who are to sponsor her for the London season, when her aunt is taken ill en route. However, she meets the attractive Anthony Davenport, and his scheming sister Pamela, who take Bella to London in their private coach. Then Bella encounters the mysterious Mr Montcalm, whom Anthony warns her away from. Yet Montcalm seems to be following her . . . Will Bella and Anthony overcome the machinations of his relatives and find love?